William Horwood

CALLANISH

ALLEN LANE

ALLEN LANE
Penguin Books Ltd
536 King's Road
London SW10 0UH

First published 1984

Set in VIP Palatino
Typeset, printed and bound in Great Britain by
Hazell Watson & Viney Limited,
Member of the BPCC Group,
Aylesbury, Bucks

BRITISH LIBRARY CATALOGUING IN PUBLICATION DATA

Horwood, William
Callanish.
I. Title
823'.914|F| PR6058.0719

ISBN 0-7139-1684-2

CONTENTS

This story is dedicated to Goldie,
the golden eagle who has been in the Cages
of London Zoo since 1959.
He escaped briefly into Regent's Park in 1965
but was finally lured back . . . and to
his fellow-captive the Cheriway carrion hawk,
an inmate of the Cages since 1932 . . .

PROLOGUE

The cage was too small for the eagle to spread his wings for balance as the journey continued southwards. He was tossed and thrown from one side to another with the frightening vibrations of the great unnatural machine that carried him as his only company.

He could not see out of the cage, for its sides were not barred but solid. But at the top along its edge there were slits sufficient for him to peer from and see the light and objects in the free world outside, if only confusedly and at strange angles. A wall of dark metal inches away from the cage restricted any real view he might have had, but it caught the daylight in its dull surface, and its continuous changes in tone and intensity mirrored the remorseless passage of the journey.

From the occasional clues of reflected sunlight that he got, and from some deeper instinct, he deduced that he was being taken away from his northern homeland.

But what it was that carried his cage, whether car or train or aeroplane, he did not know. These things were strangers to him then. He knew only that it was man-made, and stressed with an awesome power of vibration, sound and smell that had made him panic and try desperately to break out of his darkened cell when it first started to move. But there was no grip for beak or talon, no weakness that the power of his great wings could exploit.

So with sight and space taken from him he felt vulnerable and the initial fear and aggression began to give way to a pathetic abjectness. In the lonely darkness of his cage his head began to bow, his wings to droop and sag, and his proud gaze to falter into a look of hopeless despair.

Sometimes, the journeying would temporarily halt and the sounds change and grow quieter as he heard doors opening, human voices, and objects being moved.

Then an impulse of remnant aggression made him try again to peer through the tiny openings in the cage to see what was happening, from some vain hope that seeing would bring relief. But however hard he pressed his head against the side or top of the cage to get a wider view it was still too restricted to see anything that made sense to him.

Yet, bewildered as he was, and much as he needed all his courage to master the fear he felt, he retained a distant hope that after so many months the dreadful thing that had happened was coming to an end. He hoped, though he hardly dared even admit it to himself, that his instincts were wrong and that, after all, they were taking him back to the place they had taken him from, where the moors were open and wild and the great sky rose up to greet an eagle's wings. The terrible days past, when he had been confined in a place where he could not even see the sky, and where men came and looked at him and spoke in ugly voices; where the food seemed old and the air stale ... these things would be forgotten in that one single moment that was now his greatest dream: to open out his wings as an eagle should, and fly to the welcoming sky.

This distant hope gave him courage now and, as he huddled inside the carrier cage with its walls pressing in on him from all sides, he thought only of the freedom that might after all be coming. For surely the nightmare must be ending at last.

The journey rattled on; the reflected light through the cracks in the cage becoming duller and darker as the long hours passed by. He sensed that evening was approaching.

Then the quality of light and sound from outside steadily changed. He stirred himself from the posture of submission into which he had fallen again to peer out of the slits in the cage once more. The light was now unnatural, the reflections harsher and less smooth than those of natural light earlier in the journey. Worse, there were sounds of other man-machines, of engines accelerating, and a strange and choking smell to the air. Sudden noises reverberated terrifyingly in his cage.

Then the movement stopped. The vibrations of the engine ceased. He had arrived. There were bewildering noises as objects around him were moved and the top of the cage was opened. Men's faces peered in at him, their eyes grotesquely big. Then darkness again as the lid was closed, and silence, as, for a long time, no man came. It seemed like that for hours, until he was tired and despairing and it seemed that anything, even pain and death, might be better than waiting. The dim light dulled down into darkness.

Then metal doors opened again, the cage being picked up, harsh voices, and sudden swinging movement. Up into the air, the sound of feet on a gravel path, a different, quieter journey. But strangely more ominous.

If it had been only fear he had felt until then he had cause to let terror overtake him now. For suddenly, from near by, came the grim roaring of an animal that he had never heard before. It made him terribly afraid, for in its alien sound he sensed for the first time a profound imprisonment; not of the kind he had suffered these last days but of a more terrible permanent kind. The cry of an animal that has lost the wild freedom that gives it life, and yet, terribly, still lives. Then fetid smells came into his cage; and the harsh call and cawing of alien birds.

The cage lurched slightly, he slipped to one side of it, the slit at the top seemed slightly wider, and he saw for the first time, in an evening light made unnaturally bright by electric lights, the place they had brought him to.

Cages; great cages all around. But especially ahead, in the direction towards which he was being carried, a whole black line of them stood gaunt and terrible, and waiting. He looked along them and saw the most frightening sight he had ever seen: eagle after despairing eagle, staring pathetically out from behind black bars. He was being carried towards them, to join them. He struggled in utter desperation to open his wings but the cage was too small. The cries and calls of trapped creatures seemed suddenly to be all about him. The leering face of a black animal with hair that might, just might, once have been a man. It swung up into its cage and just before it disappeared it stopped and looked down at him, scratching itself with a grin on its face.

The black cliff of cages coming nearer. Eagles were staring towards him, one after another, after another. Nearer and nearer. His wings painful in their vain effort to break the carrier cage that restrained him.

Keys at a metal door. A door being opened. His cage placed on the ground. The cage's top being opened and hands reaching carefully down to him and he trying to see as light flooded in again and blinded him.

He was picked up and placed on a bare concrete floor. The carrier cage was taken away. The men stood high above him, their great eyes staring down and their white fleshy hands huge at their sides. Their legs turned away. Keys at the door and it clanked shut. And now a bigger cage around him beyond whose harsh black bars he could see the evening sky, grey and lowering, a sky into whose freedom he had dreamed of flying; a dream that had kept him alive.

He knew instinctively that wherever he was it was permanent. There was the feel of living death all around, and the eyes of the creatures staring at him seemed to have lost touch for ever with the liberty that had first given them life. He raised his wings, rose off the floor of his cage, and in one huge despairing useless gesture, dashed his talons against its bars, his eyes staring up hopelessly at the sky he could never reach; his heart beginning already to die for loss of the freedom that, he sensed, had been taken from him for ever.

PART ONE

THE CAGES

1

The howl of a wolf rose into the cold evening air of London. It faded away for a few seconds before starting again as others joined it, their howls hanging eerily in the cold shadows of the trees of Regent's Park, before dying down again among the bars and cages of London Zoo.

The young eagle trembled with fear, and then shivered with cold and loneliness as he looked at the cage that surrounded him, and above to where the bars and wire mesh stood out harshly against the lowering sky. A bitter wind scurried among the branches of the trees that rose above and behind the stark line of old-fashioned eagle cages.

A voice came from out of the dark depths of the cage to his right.

'What is your name?' it asked. The voice was faint and troubled, and sounded like that of an old female eagle.

When they had carried him into his cage that afternoon and taken him out of the carrier box in which he had journeyed for so long, he had hardly dared to look around him at the other cages. But he had finally done so and had seen other eagles, each in his own cage, all mature, all seeming big and threatening. Most had ignored him, some had ruffled and flown in their cages from side to side, clashing their great talons on the bars to intimidate him.

But in the cage next to his, from where the voice now came, he had seen nothing. Whatever eagle was there was hidden inside the rough concrete shelter that provided the only escape in the Victorian metal cages from prying eyes.

'What is your name?' The voice came again out of the
darkness and seemed stronger now.

'My name is Creggan,' he whispered. 'I am a golden eagle.'

'I know. I could see that when you arrived, Creggan.' There
was a long silence then and Creggan waited, not sure what to
do or say. He felt unsafe and alone, as if whatever he did
would be wrong. A wolf howled again, and then others joined
it until the very cage he was in seemed full of the lonely
howls of lost trapped animals.

'What is that sound?' Creggan asked, doing his best to
seem merely curious but unable to stop the fear he felt from
creeping into his voice.

'The wolves. Their enclosure is near by, at the back of our
cages, and though it is impossible to see them we often hear
them.' She had a strange voice, old and frail but full of
authority. Even though he had not seen her yet, Creggan felt
in awe of her.

'Where are you from, Creggan, and what is it that you fear
in this place?' She spoke almost as if she could read his mind.

'I'm not afraid,' said Creggan angrily, ruffling his wings in
the way he thought adult eagles might do when they wanted
to look unconcerned. But the voice that had spoken waited,
as if it knew that eventually Creggan would speak the truth.
The night began to fall cold and silent about them.

'I don't know where I'm from,' said Creggan eventually,
and rather more meekly. 'I can't remember . . . something
was put over my head and eyes and I could not see . . .'

'You *must* remember . . .' she replied. 'Now, *where are you
from?*' Her voice was suddenly stronger, and it was angry
now.

Creggan felt even more afraid, not of the strangeness and
unfamiliarity of the dreadful place to which he had been
brought, but of the eagle in the cage next to his.

'I don't know . . .' he faltered again. 'I can't remember . . .'

It was true, he no longer seemed able to. All he seemed to
remember was being on the edge of a great nest of sticks with

a scatter of rabbit carcases about him, and a loch and a beautiful glen stretching far below, green, brown, distant. His mother was hunting, his father watching from a rock a little way off, and Creggan was trying to win food from his bigger stronger sibling, another male, who had been born before him. Though his downy feathers were beginning to strengthen, he felt weak and vulnerable, for he never seemed to get enough food, or be able to beat off the brutal and painful pecks of his sibling from whom, by some ancient lore of eagles, his parents did not protect him. He could sense that his parents despaired of him and were beginning to put their efforts into his stronger rival and that soon . . . But that day his mother had suddenly flown a warning flight, while his father rose into the air and swooped into the valley and back beneath the cliff edge, and suddenly a man was there with something green in his hand which rose into the sky above him and came down towards him. Only him. The last he saw was a gloat in his sibling's eyes, and a final, spiteful, vengeful lunge in his direction before he was taken away.

Thinking back now, Creggan could still hear the calls of anger and alarm of his parents, as he hissed at the man coming at him and tried to strike at his hands with his beak and talons. But the hands came cunning and swift and raised a harsh green fabric up, until there was darkness over his head and he was paralysed with fear as he was lifted up and began a long and terrible journey. The sound of his parents' calls were muffled and then grew distant and all he could hear was the rough footfall of the man on the rocks and scree and the sound of his breathing . . .

Then months of lonely captivity in a small cage in a closed place where the wind did not blow, and other men came and examined him and time passing into blankness. Then a new journey into light and noise and he had come to where he was now.

He found he had been speaking the memory out into the night and among the bleak cages around. He could see by the dark light that came down from the night sky, a sky that glowed with vivid city lights, that on stands in nearby cages other eagles were listening to his story and staring at him silently.

There was movement in the cage from where the old female's voice came and a shadow came out on the floor of her cage, thin and gaunt, the silhouette of an eagle. It was still, but he sensed her staring at him from out of the darkness of her shelter, and a laboured and painful breathing came from her. Creggan was afraid.

'What was the name of the place where you were born? What was its direction?'

'North. But its name . . . I don't know,' he said again. Because he wanted to forget that place to which, some terrible fear told him, he would never return. He wanted to lose it from his memory. But the dark shape of the old eagle in the cage next to him stayed still, waiting, staring, willing him to talk.

The silence of the night deepened as the strange and alien animals of the Zoo fell asleep. In a cage near Creggan an eagle shook its feathers; somewhere talons rasped briefly on metal and were still. The trees high above the cages whispered and were silent.

Creggan had never in his short life felt so desolate, and try as he did he could not rest and fall asleep. He had hoped that the new journey he had made would be to freedom, back to his beloved homesite and his parents.

But he could sense that this place was permanent, it was his home. And he felt the strange eagle in the cage next to his waiting for a reply to her question about where he had come from. There are few more important questions than that for an eagle to answer.

He thought back and . . . and it was all so confused and seemed so long ago. His parents had only just begun to give him and his sibling the lore of their territory, telling him the names of eagles who had nested there before.

He remembered staring out from the nest site on a clear cold morning and seeing a line of grey-blue a few miles to the north which they said was the sea. He could see cliffs and a distant wash of white. It was called Cape Wrath, they said. One day he would fly to it, and beyond, over the sea. When he did he could call himself a Wrath eagle, for the site he had been born to was that of the proudest and fiercest of the golden eagles of Scotland and his mother was a Wrath eagle before him, his father having flown up from the south and won his place at her side in aerial combat with other males.

One day he had asked his parents if the Wrath eagles were the greatest of the golden eagles, and after a long pause his mother said, 'No eagle is greater than another, all of us are the same wherever we come from and whatever kind we are. For there are many kinds of eagles, Creggan, many kinds.'

But later his father had said, 'But though the site of Cape Wrath is one of the greatest sites, yet there is one other which is revered among golden eagles above them all. Not for the power of the flight of the eagles that come from there, or their cunning or aggressiveness. No, they are revered for the power of spirit.'

'Spirit?' he had asked. 'What is that? Can anything be more powerful than flight? And what is the site of these eagles called?'

'One day you will understand the nature of the power of those eagles and why their name is spoken in awe by each one of us. Their site is over the sea west of Wrath, at the eastern side of the Isle of Lewis. Its name is Callanish and eagles from it should be honoured. Their powers are great.'

This was some of the lore Creggan remembered and he found himself whispering aloud in the night . . . 'Cape Wrath, I come from near there. Cape Wrath. When I fly out from the nest over the moors to its great and awesome cliffs and gyre on the winds out over the sea then can I call myself a Wrath eagle.'

As he found himself speaking out the name into the

imprisoned night of the Zoo he wanted to cry out with sadness. And that he felt an eagle should not do.

'Cape Wrath. So you came from Cape Wrath . . .' It was the old female eagle speaking from the darkness near him, repeating the name he had finally spoken. She sounded more friendly than she had before, but her voice still carried awesome authority.

'Where did *you* come from?' he whispered in his misery.

She was silent, and he was beginning to grow tired. His fear was beginning to leave him, for in her unseen presence there was a kind of powerful peace.

'I am of Callanish,' she said simply. 'That was my homesite.'

Callanish! An eagle of Callanish! And now Creggan did begin to feel an awe and a deeper fear, for this grim place must be strong indeed to hold an eagle from the sacred site of Callanish.

'But . . .' he began.

But she interrupted him softly, her words gentle and her spirit as powerful as the strongest wind.

'There is time enough yet to tell you of that,' she said. 'I am tired now and must rest. But I needed to be sure that you had not forgotten your homesite. You must never forget it. For if you are to survive here you will need to remember it, even though you will finally want to forget. But I shall not let you. As long as I am here to remind you I shall never let you forget.

'Forgetting is the greatest weakness, and your greatest enemy. Most of the eagles in the Cages have forgotten, for they cannot bear to remember, and because of that even if the opportunity came they would not be able to return to their homesites. But there are a few here, a very few, who cannot forget, and in them there is courage still, and strength, waiting, waiting . . . In time you will learn which ones they are. For myself, I am perhaps too old now to hope to return.

But not too old that I cannot make sure that you never forget. NEVER.'

The word came from her with sudden and frightening force and it seemed to Creggan as if it was a burden he would carry always in this place. But then her voice softened as she whispered, 'Now you must rest, only rest, for there will be much for you to learn and we cannot say how quickly or slowly time will pass.'

She sounded tired but, though her breathing was laboured and painful, it seemed to Creggan now that her voice was the only friendly thing left in his world. It drifted and swirled about him, making him peaceful and tired, until his sense of loss began to go and the night was no longer awesome, for he had the protection of a Callanish eagle near him, and that gave him peace to rest and sleep at last . . .

2

The following morning Creggan was roused from half-sleep by the loud and urgent calling of an eagle. The sound was so alarming that the ducks on the lake enclosure opposite rose up into the air in sudden flight.

The calls, which were in an exceptionally rough and harsh voice, came from an eagle in the cage beyond the one from which the old female had spoken in the night. He was of a kind Creggan did not recognize, with white head plumage that ran magnificently down his neck, and wing feathers of a deep and rich brown and a black-yellow beak.

But what struck Creggan most of all was the fierceness of his expression. There was great pride in his stance and he had a strange and frightening way of pulling his head right back over his body when he made one of his series of calls. And had his voice been able to cut through metal as it cut through the early morning air, then they would all of them have been free of the Cages in moments.

The eagle was clinging with his talons to the wall of the old female's cage and seemed to be looking into it as if to work out where she had gone. For there was about her cage a silence and stillness so great that it seemed as if she had disappeared.

After a time he began to whisper in a voice that tried now to be soft and gentle, in complete contrast to his alarm calls: 'Come on, Minch, you can't really be so ill that you can't show me your face just for a moment, or let me hear the ruffle of one of your wings. I know we've argued all these years and I've been irritable, if not downright rude, but . . . but . . .' and

Creggan was astonished to see that this fiercest of eagles was suddenly close to a profound grief and for a few moments quite unable to say anything more. He just stared into the dreadful dark depths of the old female's shelter waiting hopelessly for some sign that she was alive. But there was only silence to answer him.

Suddenly the eagle opened his wings, fell back in an arc of restricted flight, and dashed his talons on the far side of his cage before plunging back towards Creggan, so powerfully and full of anger that it was as if he had forgotten that there were two walls of bars and iron mesh between them. Creggan involuntarily drew back in fear and alarm.

'What are you looking at?' cried the eagle at Creggan. 'How dare you stare like that? Aren't you satisfied that you're going to get what you want? She's dying and you'll be the only golden eagle here then and *won't* that be nice!' Creggan stared at the eagle blankly as he continued, 'Don't pretend you don't know. She's a golden eagle like you and because she's dying they've brought you here to replace her. Well, you never will, you never can. She was the strongest of us all, the wisest and the kindest – she gave hope to the sad and courage to the weak. You cannot replace her!'

Then he ran back along the bare wooden branch that hung across his cage and turning suddenly, raised his wings in the air and lunged forward towards Creggan again. He brought his talons and beak down on the bars with such force that the very Cages themselves shook with the power of it.

Even if direct physical assault was made impossible by the bars of the cages there was something about this sudden attack on Creggan that replaced the fear he had felt earlier with anger. He might still only be a juvenile who had never flown freely on the wind but he felt he had done nothing to warrant the abuse and fury of an eagle whose name he did not even know.

So he raised his wings, which still bore the light-coloured plumage of a juvenile, reared up his head in as fierce a way as he could, and called out, 'I did not choose to come to this miserable place, or to live with ones such as you who grow angry at nothing, or nothing I can understand. I cannot . . .' but he could not go on because his voice was shaking with such rage.

Instead he raised his talons and struck at the wire mesh in his own turn, which only provoked the other eagle to do the same again, the sounds of both of them increased by the flapping of their great wings and the crashing of their beaks on the cage walls as they vainly tried to get at each other.

They were both so angry that they did not immediately see the movement that came from the old female's shelter in the cage between them. From out of the darkness at the back of her cage came the slow and ailing movement of a wing; then the drag of a weak old talon, then the hunch of a back that was grey and dry with age and illness; and finally in the archway of the shelter entrance where the dank morning light fell, the aged and troubled form of an eagle.

She stared up from the ground, her wings hanging loose as if she no longer had strength to hold them to her body, her left wing seeming bent as if it had once been broken. She did not have sufficient strength to take stance on the gaunt bare branch above her head nor had she touched the remnant of meat that had been left the day before as her food and which now lay on the ground at her side.

Her face was racked with pain and it was clear that she was very ill. But there was something in her gaze, some power of kindness and peace, that would have stilled the very sky itself of stormy winds and rain. And now it stilled Creggan, and it brought silence to the other eagle.

'I do not like . . .' she whispered in a voice so quiet that it brought both of them lower in their cages to get nearer to her, the argument between them forgotten, '. . . I do not like to see eagles fighting in this way over something that is no eagle's fault. You, Creggan, must never visit your anger on other eagles, but only on this . . .' And with the slightest bend of her head she indicated the Zoo around them beyond the Cages and all the incarcerated creatures it contained.

'And you, Kraal of the distant South, must try to remember all I have taught you these long years and pass it on. For surely a time will come when what I have said will happen *will* happen, and then one among us eagles will fly freely on the wind. And whichever one it is will fly for all of us, transforming at last the loss and suffering we have felt these years into the power and hope of purposeful flight.'

She stared away from them and up beyond the cage towards the grey sky, and Creggan saw in her eyes a longing and a hope that he sensed had been with her all her long life, and was with her even now when he saw she was so near death. He noticed too that for the first time since he had arrived at the Cages there was a total silence, as if all the eagles, and all the imprisoned creatures thereabout had instinctively understood that this old eagle's troubled painful words marked an end to a terrible life; and perhaps in some strange way the beginning of something none dared hope might come to pass.

Then the silence was broken by the sound of metal on metal at the far end of the Cages and of a gate being opened, followed by the heavy remorseless tread of Men's feet.

'The Keepers are coming,' whispered Kraal. 'It is not their usual time. Are they finally coming for you, Minch?' He spoke with awe and fear in his voice, and as if he believed that only Minch herself among all of them could know and understand what might be in Men's minds.

The old female bent her head low and nodded.

'Yes, they are coming for me now, and my time may be over. This moment has been so long in coming, and yet I had thought that perhaps I might, just once . . . just once . . .'

With difficulty she stared up again at the unreachable sky beyond the bars and wire mesh of her cage and though she tried to say more she was unable to, for her wings sagged ever more weakly and she seemed barely able to hold up her head. While her eyes, which had been so clear and proud, seemed tired now and were beginning to fade.

'With help from another I might have survived. With help . . .' and her whispered words were so quiet that only Creggan and Kraal heard them.

'What can we do, old friend?' cried out Kraal. 'Tell us what we can do!' And he mantled his wings hugely at the approaching Men, calling out angrily at them with his harsh voice.

So that it was only Creggan who heard old Minch's final words: 'Help lies beyond the power of our wings and strength, it goes where our spirit goes. But mine is tired now, so very tired. When an eagle loses hope then death is near.' Her voice faded as her body weakened and drooped, so that she seemed no more than the shadow of the eagle she must once have been, and a shadow that was losing itself in the darkness of a cage.

Then the Men came. Two of them. Noisily opening the door in front of her and carrying a small portable cage from which Creggan instinctively flinched in fear. It was the same kind as he had once been kept in for so long.

The Men's giant heads and great white hands bent over old Minch and their voices muttered deeply. They pulled back one of her wings, they examined her talons, and she did not struggle. Then one of them put her in the carrier cage and took her out while the other closed the door on her empty cage.

Then Kraal raised his head and let out a terrible call and shriek of sadness. And all along the Cages the other eagles scuttered and muttered, some staring silently at the Men taking the oldest and most venerable among them away, others pretending not to look.

As the Men carried Minch away Creggan looked desperately about him as if to seek out some inspiration for the action and sign of hope that her final words had seemed to wish to invoke. He looked at Kraal, who called out in loss and anger, and at the other eagles up and down the Cages, as if somewhere there there might be some help.

It was in that terrible moment of loss that he noticed for the first time the eagle in the cage on the other side of his from where Minch's cage was. It was another female, but small and insignificant-looking, with tawny wings whose gloss had faded. She was staring at Creggan from the top of her cage and appeared to be trying to say something.

'No good expecting *her* to talk. She hasn't spoken since the day she got here, I'm told, and that's long before my time,' said Kraal aggressively. 'Much good you are, Slorne, or will ever be!'

And yet for all her beaten and pathetic appearance it seemed to Creggan there was in this eagle Slorne's eyes something that Creggan saw nowhere else in the Cages at that moment: purpose. A possibility. And whatever it was, Slorne now tried to communicate it to Creggan. But though her mouth opened it was a silent entreaty and all she seemed able to do was cling to the top of her cage near where branches of trees hung and vainly try to say words that would not come.

'What is it?' asked Creggan desperately, watching where Minch was being taken away. 'There is something I can do, isn't there, Slorne? You know of something. Tell me if you can.'

Slorne turned away and stared out through the top of her cage as if to say, 'There, where the skies are, where the great clouds drift and the winds blow endlessly through time, seek there and you will find what Minch needs.' And Creggan followed her helpless gaze, out past the bars to the great sky itself and it seemed that direction came suddenly to him at last. He felt the power of the winds in his wings until some hope, some purpose, came into him. He felt again the space and size of the moorland landscape that had, so briefly, been his natural home. He felt in himself the freedom that Minch, in her whispered final words, had seemed to begin to forget, and he remembered the words of his parents: 'One day you will understand the nature of the power of those eagles . . . those eagles of Callanish . . . honour their power, *believe* in them . . .'

Believe in them . . . was that the whispered silent thing that Minch needed in this darkest hour? Then did Creggan turn from the sight of the sky to which Slorne had directed him and back to the reality of the final taking of Minch of Callanish. And he mantled his wings and reared up his head and it was not whispers or meekness or acceptance that came from him. For he cried out with power and anger, a cry so loud and full of authority that the Men themselves stopped and looked back in surprise.

'There is no need for sadness or shame, Kraal!' were the words he spoke, not knowing where the thoughts in his mind were coming from. 'There is no need for hopelessness, no need for pity or despair among any of us, for Minch is not going to die. She is an eagle of a special kind, strong and powerful and she still has enough power to put her strength in *my* wings. She will *not* die. She will come back and give us all the strength we need.'

'But once the Men take an eagle like that they never come back, never,' said Kraal, his great voice faltering before the power of Creggan's.

'Then the fact that she *will* will be a sign to us that the hope she gives is not in vain. And why should she not come back? Do none of you know who she is?'

He found now he was speaking to all the eagles in the Cages and that they were listening to him. And as he spoke a memory was coming back of words his mother had spoken to him when she had talked of the lore of the golden eagles of Scotland. It was the memory of what they had told him of Callanish, and of the eagles that came from there.

'Minch is not just any eagle, she is an eagle of Callanish where the greatest of our kind come from. She carries in her wings great power and mystery even though she has been cast in these Cages for so long. A Callanish eagle can never die here but only within sight of that great place from which she comes!'

Creggan could not see that at the sound of his words and particularly at the name of Callanish, there came into the eyes of old Minch, who was now held in the cage by the Men, a look as from some vast distance in the past. It came from where memory is young and the power in a young eagle's flight is great and can never fade. His words brought to her eyes the same look that is in an eagle's eyes as she flies again above moorland of the Western Isles and watches, far below, her own shadow flighting across the wild moorland wastes of Callanish.

Nor could Creggan see that with that return of some sense of a spirit of life that can never die there came to the nearly lifeless wings of the close-caged Minch a sudden struggle and slight flutter of purpose – not much, but enough to make the Man look down in surprise and tighten his grip on the carrier cage. Then the Men were gone out of sight.

Creggan called out once more after her, powerfully, and Kraal stared at him in silent surprise and just a little awe, while unnoticed by any of them the meek Slorne relaxed a little and seemed to nod her head, as if to whisper to a waiting sky, 'Yes . . . yes . . . yes.'

Then, as Creggan abruptly turned and went down into the silence and gloom of his shelter, where no other eagle could see him and he could be alone with his thoughts, Kraal muttered after him, 'Golden eagle! Your kind are strange. You find hope even in the shadow of death.'

But there was respect in his voice as he added, 'From where does your great strength come? Old Minch had it and you seem to have it as well, Creggan. Does it come from this place Callanish that you both tell of?'

But Creggan did not hear him. In the silence of his shelter he was finally letting the true sorrow he felt for all that had happened in the last months come into him, and he was beginning to grieve. For fine and powerful though his words were, they had seemed to come from beyond him and here, now, alone in this miserable place, with Minch gone from the Cages, he was already doubting the truth of what he had said only moments before. And grief and deep despair were a cold wind whose power he could no longer fight against . . .

3

In the next few days Creggan began to learn about the Zoo in which he was now imprisoned. Some of it Kraal told him; other things he could see for himself.

The Cages formed a long connected line facing west. Their bars and wire mesh were painted black and though some were smaller than others they were all designed the same. Each had a cracked and grubby-looking concrete floor lined with a layer of shingle, a concrete shelter for retreat, one or two bare branches to act as a place to take stance; and in most there was a small pool of water for cleaning and drinking.

The Men usually came twice a day – once to clean out the Cages and once to feed the eagles. The food was good, fresh meat and bone, but though it was better than anything Creggan had had since he had been caught, nothing ever seemed to taste as good as the food he remembered from his homesite.

Opposite the Cages was what the eagles called the Three Island Pond where ducks and flamingos were kept. Creggan watched them hour after hour, envying their freedom in such a wide area, though a small ditch right round the pond prevented the ducks wandering too far from its edge. But there were trees on the islands which filled with sunlight in the morning and made a pleasant contrast to the concrete and bars of so much of the Zoo.

To the left of them was a complex of nets and cages in which the leopards, lions, cheetahs and tigers lived. If it could be called living. They too came from the land to the south

where Kraal and Slorne came from and their colours were
bright and striking.

Even from the distance of the Cages Creggan could see that
they were not content. The tiger that was nearest to him, and
which he could see most easily, seemed so bored that he did
the same thing day after day, hour after hour. Instead of
staring blankly out at the world, or nervously striking at the
fence, as some of the eagles did, he trekked back and forth in
a figure of eight over an area that was only one tiny part of
his caged area. Forward eight steps and round, back eight
steps and round, forward . . . hour after tedious hour, the
grass beneath his feet worn brown and bare by his terrible
pacing. Occasionally, especially in the evenings, Creggan
would see him stop and roar until he could roar no more; and
then he would continue pacing, on and on. And on.

But if Creggan's own sense of imprisonment was made
worse by the sight of other caged creatures, it was heightened
yet further by the fact that small song birds like sparrows,
thrushes and starlings would dart freely in between the bars
of the Cages and take advantage of what they found there.

Some simply washed in the pool of water meant for each
eagle, dipping their heads and wings in and letting the water
run down their backs. Others dived and scurried for any food
they found – sometimes a speck of meat from the eagles' own
food, or perhaps the crumbs from some piece of bread that
the visitors to the Zoo wrongly threw in.

At first Creggan had mantled at these free birds, raising his
great wings and lunging his beak towards them in a threatening way. But they took no notice. He soon found out why. If
ever he tried to do more – to hop or semi-fly down towards
them to try to catch them – they simply darted away and out
of reach.

After only a few days he gave up and did his best to ignore
them even though they had the one thing above all he was
beginning to want: freedom.

*

Creggan had been afraid of almost everything when he first came – of the Men, of the strange sounds from the rest of the Zoo, of the people staring from the path that ran past the Cages. But very soon he got used to these things and learnt to understand what they meant. Most of all he learnt that there was no danger. None. The eagles were safe from all harm. Nobody and nothing could get at them.

'. . . and that is the greatest danger, according to Minch,' Kraal told him one day, concluding a brief account of what life in the Cages was like. 'Of course you wouldn't understand *that* because you haven't been here long enough.'

Although Kraal tried his hardest to do as Minch had told him and talk to Creggan, the fact was that he was not very good at it. For one thing he was an impatient sort of eagle, inclined to get angry and feel insulted at the smallest thing; for another – and this took Creggan a while to realize – he was preoccupied with thinking about what had happened to Minch, not daring to hope that what Creggan had so boldly said about her coming back was true. As the days had gone by and there had been no sign of her, Kraal had become more and more convinced that Creggan's belief in her return was hopeless and that Minch was gone for ever.

But as the days stretched into tedious weeks Creggan found strange comfort in the silent presence of Slorne in the adjacent cage. Slorne would emerge from her retreat each dawn to take stance in a high corner of her cage, the same place she had been when the Men took Minch away. From there she would stare hour after hour through the branches of the trees above as they swayed against the ever-changing sky, as if she was waiting to catch a glimpse of something precious she had lost a lifetime before. And though there was something immeasurably sad about this hopeless daily wait, yet sometimes, just briefly, Creggan would catch her looking in his direction in a way that spoke of support and encouragement.

'*You* think she'll come back, don't you, Slorne?' whispered Creggan late one evening as dusk settled miserably over the

Cages. There was no immediate sign of an answer, but after
Creggan had given up any hope of a reply and was looking
at the path lights beginning to come on in the Park outside
the Zoo there was a subtle shift of talons in Slorne's cage, a
gentle shift of wings, the swiftest of meek glances, and
Creggan, too late to catch the look full on, yet sensed that in
her mute way Slorne was saying 'Yes, oh yes, you were right
to predict her return.' This knowledge that another eagle
there believed his prediction had been right gave Creggan
comfort in those first weeks in the Cages.

So when one day Kraal was mocking Slorne for her silent
uselessness, Creggan was forced to say in her defence that
perhaps the silence only hid an eagle who was kind and
gentle and whose talons carried no harm for any eagle there.

'Well, she may seem like that now,' said Kraal one evening,
'but you wait till the autumn comes and the swifts and
swallows start flocking before they begin their winter migration. You won't call her peaceful then!'

'Why, what does she do?' asked Creggan.

'Do? It's what she doesn't do you want to think about. She
flies back and forth in her cage as much as it's possible,
dashing her talons against the bars and hitting her beak
against the top. You may think *I'm* bad enough, but Slorne! I
don't envy you having her cage next to yours. The only eagle
who can settle her is Minch . . . *was* Minch I should say,' he
added sadly.

Then he continued: 'Minch could say the right things. The
lammergeyer that was where you are now, who died after
only three years, he wasn't any good at all. Only made her
worse. Minch would have to shut him up and calm down
Slorne herself until eventually she would quieten herself
down and let the rest of us get some peace and quiet.'

'Where does she come from?'

'Same as me: from the South, over a great blue sea called
the Mediterranean. Beyond that sea rises a mountain range
and beyond that stretches a vast desert where the sun twists

round and beats down so hot it would dry out an eagle's wings and turn them to dust if he flew too long. There the air rises hotly and on it an eagle may soar further south to where Slorne's kind live, and where my kind come from too.'

A sun so hot it would dry out an eagle's wings! Creggan was fascinated by this thought and wanted Kraal to tell him more about this place. But he would not. Indeed, Creggan soon found out that none of the eagles seemed to like talking about where they came from or how they came to be in the Cages.

As the days passed Creggan got used to Slorne's silence and grew to like it and he would perch at his stance and think about the land in the South where the two of them came from and try to imagine what it was like.

Then he would remember his own beloved homesite, and whisper to himself of its dour moorland and rough sea coast, and the winds and the rain that did battle with an eagle's wings. Then, pretending for a moment that he was back there, he would turn round and face the back of his cage, open his wings, and glide down the few feet to where his food lay on the ground, pretending that it was prey and that the few feet was hundreds of feet, and that he could feel strong winds on his wings and was an adult eagle, and free, free to fly where he liked.

There were several Men who regularly came in and out of the Cages to clean and feed the eagles. All were firm but kind with the eagles, who were passive in return, but for a very few like Kraal, who gave them as much trouble as he could. Creggan followed suit and made it as difficult as possible for the Men to handle him.

There was however one inmate of the Cages who never caused the Men trouble – perhaps because he was not an eagle at all – and that was Woil, a buzzard whose cage was just beyond Slorne's.

When the Men came Woil would simper and whisper his

pleasure and let them handle him as they liked as he said such things as: 'Nice Man, pleasant person. Oh yes, I do not mind for I like to be good. Nice person, pleasant Man.'

Though the Men could not understand a single one of these sickening and servile words, it seemed to work, for some occasionally gave Woil especially pleasant portions of food and all seemed to appreciate how easy it was to handle him.

'Don't you listen to Woil, 'cos given half a chance he'll tell you all sorts of nonsense that no eagle should listen to,' Kraal said when Woil first started talking like this after Creggan's arrival.

'Of course you wouldn't like him anyway from what I hear about where you come from. *Buzzards!* It's like my kind in the South and the vultures.' Kraal was referring to the fact that in Scotland golden eagles are enemies of the buzzard, whom they despise and seek to chase off their territory.

'My parents only told me a bit about them,' said Creggan, 'and I only saw one once when a pair came close to my homesite and my mother attacked them. They soon left! What are vultures like?'

'Bigger. Nastier. Cleverer. Snidier. Dirtier.' said Kraal contemptuously. 'You're lucky you're up this end of the Cages with us because there's . . .' and here he dropped his voice into a horrified whisper, '. . . there's a couple of vultures down at the other end. I had to occupy a temporary cage next to them once when mine was being repaired. Disgusting. I made such a fuss that the Keeper had to move me back here quick. Can't think what people see in them,' he added darkly, referring to the fact that most of the Zoo visitors who came by the Cages spent more time looking at the vultures than they did at African eagles like him.

So, slowly, Creggan came to learn the routine and the lore of the Zoo and, without realizing it, to let his world, which had once been so wide and full of hope and freedom, close in and grow small; a place in which the trivial things like the way Woil talked to the Men, or where the vultures were, were more important than flight, freedom, the sky and the winds they were banned from.

The weather changed for the better. Sun shone, warm breezes blew, and the plane trees behind the Cages grew greener and more leafy with each hour. On some mornings the ducks on Three Island Pond would take off in great arcing flights against the sun, round and behind the Cages and out of sight, round again and behind the distant trees and then suddenly back again as if it had all been a mistake and they had never meant to fly off in the first place.

There were many kinds and each day he seemed to notice more. Creggan recognized some, like the mallard, the tufted duck, and the moorhen, but others Kraal would have to identify for him until he knew their names: wigeon, pintail, pochard . . . how he envied them their freedom on the pond. But he envied more the great herring gulls and black-headed gulls which he watched through the bars of his cage as they soared on the summery winds, the white and grey of their feathers caught brightly by the sun as they banked into a turn. Sometimes he would forget himself in the beauty of their flight, not understanding why people would come to see him and the other miserable eagles caged and confined and not seem to even notice the gulls and bold black rooks soaring freely and so beautifully above their heads. But there were times too when he could not bear to look at the free birds and preferred to huddle wanly in the shadows of his shelter, where no visitors could see him, and stare at the bare, stained concrete that was his wild moorland, and the grubby little basin of water that was his lake and the few square feet of cage that was his sky.

Yet Creggan did not dislike all the Men he saw. Certainly those who worked in the Cages he did not wish to like at all, but among the people who came by the Cages were some who came regularly, day after day, and they seemed all right to him. It was in the third week after Minch had gone that he had first noticed that one of the Men, older than the Keeper, regularly came to the benches that ranged along the path by the Cages, and sat down for a while. Like so many of the visitors, though he was dressed in the bright overalls of the Men he stared for long periods into the Cages, but it seemed to Creggan that his staring was different from the others and less cruel. His hair was grey, and his face lined and brown as if he had been in the sun for a long time. He usually came in the middle of the day, pushing something ahead of him which he set by the side of the benches before taking some food out of a box. He did not feed this to the eagles but sat and ate it himself, and spent more time staring into the deserted depths of Minch's cage than any other.

'We call him the Sweeper,' explained Kraal. 'In the summer he comes nearly every day and always does the same thing.'

'Why "Sweeper"?' Creggan wanted to know.

'That's what he does. His job is to clean along the paths of the Zoo and that thing he pushes is for the rubbish he collects, and along its side he has two brooms and a shovel. He used to be a Keeper years ago, though he never worked in the Cages or with any of the birds, but now he's just the Sweeper. None of us mind him at all and he used to be a special friend of Minch's.'

'Why?'

'She never told me. She just said that he was here when she first came to the Zoo and that he's been here longer than anyone else. You know what he can do?'

Creggan shook his head.

'Apart from Minch he's the only living thing can quieten Slorne in the autumn when the migrations start. Don't ask me how he does it. He just goes up to her cage and stands there, hardly even looking at her, and she quietens down quick as anything.'

So Creggan became interested in the Sweeper, and wondered if he would ever come up to his cage and say something, in the way Men did. He could sense that there was no harm in the Sweeper, and as the days went by and still Minch did not come back, he seemed to sense too that the Sweeper cared and was on his side in wishing for her safe return.

About three weeks after Minch had gone, the Sweeper came by one evening just when the Men were shutting the Zoo down for the night. He was not pushing his barrow. Instead of sitting on the benches he came right up to Minch's cage and stared into its emptiness for a long time.

Creggan sensed that something was happening, something was changing. The Sweeper reached out a hand and gently put it on the front of Minch's cage. Then he turned the few feet to Creggan's cage and stared up to where Creggan had taken stance on the bare branch of wood that hung across his cage. Creggan was not afraid but instead filled with the feeling that there was strength in the Man that was on his side; and anger too; and that something was happening, something that concerned Minch. Then the Sweeper left, and the Zoo grew quiet for the night.

As night fell Creggan thought no more of it, and retreated into his shelter to sleep. And sleep the whole night through he might have, had not he woken suddenly, for no apparent reason, into crisis. Not one he could see, or touch, or fly from; but one he could feel.

His cage was cast in a silvery light so bright that the patterns of the bars could clearly be seen as shadows on its floor. It was the moon. Everything around him was deathly still. The feeling of vague unease he had felt when the Sweeper had visited the Cages that evening now returned sharply, almost painfully, multiplied a hundred times.

Something *was* wrong, terribly wrong, and it concerned Minch. Something was happening to her and something told him she needed help. He could sense that she was alive somewhere close, where the Men had taken her, and that she was very near her end; nearer than she had been before.

Creggan came out of his shelter and into the open of his moonlit cage and looked over towards where Kraal might be. Only shadows and bars.

'Kraal!' he whispered urgently, but there was no reply.

The feeling of crisis was growing in him and he felt he could barely breathe. He turned towards where Woil was.

'Woil! Woil!' But like Kraal he seemed deep asleep.

Then there was the barest rustle of wings in the night and Creggan saw that staring at him, from the next cage, was Slorne, quite silent, but her eyes full of a terrible entreaty.

'You can feel it as well, can't you?' said Creggan. 'Something's wrong, isn't it?' But Slorne could only stare mutely at him in the cold moonlight.

'You've known Minch longer than Kraal even,' said Creggan. 'You must know what to do. Can't you tell me? Can't you speak just once?'

Slorne stared, her feathers a silvery grey in the night, and seemed to try to find some strength which would let her speak. But none came. Then she turned her head and stared to the top of her cage, and then flew darkly up to it and took her usual stance staring up, up now towards the moon and distant stars. But occasionally she stared back at him and then up again, as she had sometimes before, except that this time, with the sense of crisis and danger hanging over the Cages, it seemed there was something urgent about her stance and her stares.

'You're telling me something, aren't you,' whispered Creggan, 'something I can do. Something out there I can . . . I can . . .' but the words were stopped in him and he seemed to suffocate and gasp with the sense of a power beyond the Cages that he had sensed briefly before. It was as if some great mass of thunder-cloud was driving up and up, and darkening the sky before it broke into wind and storm and rain; except that the night was clear and the only movement was the slight rustle of the branches above, silvered against the stars by the moon's bright light.

Then from out there where Slorne's gaze had led him, from out of the dark moonlit sky, there came a distant calling of a name, a place, a power, and it was like a great presence he could only *feel* and not see, and it cast itself over him, and over his cage, and over the whole Zoo, and over more than that. It made him see that before its power all of this was nothing and yet, at the same time, without him, or Slorne, or Minch or any of the creatures, imprisoned and free, its power would be nothing. And he was in awe before the sense that its power was in him, and yet he was nothing; and yet again, perhaps, if only he knew how, that power might help him . . .

Then words, distant and unknown to him, began to form in him and to speak through him, and a name loomed before him as if he could feel the place it represented; and the name was Callanish. Most sacred of the sites, the place where Minch had come from.

'Creggan! Creggan!' the powers in the night seemed to call, 'she is alone and needs to know you are near. She must come to sense that you are close by and believe in her . . .'

Then he raised his wings and lifted himself up as Slorne had done to the very top of his cage. Grasping the side of the cage with his talons he fixed his stare on the night sky above where moonlit clouds moved slowly across stars. He put his head as near the bars as he could so that they did not obstruct his view. He wanted to stare at a free sky.

Then he whispered 'Callanish, Callanish, from you come the greatest of our kind and the strongest, and none of yours can die here. Let her find strength to survive this dark night, for I know she is near to death itself. Let her survive. And if you grant it and have her return then will I help her be free, even before myself. For her life is more important than mine and all my kind do honour her. Even before myself will I see that she goes free.' Then he fell silent, as if he was thinking of some way to turn this promise into a purpose, and he added, in the barest of trembled whispers, 'As I am an eagle of Wrath do I promise it. She will go free before I do and so long as she is captive will I be. This is my vow.'

Then Creggan fell silent staring into the night, as Slorne did near by. Then he looked across at her and, though she was silent, still he knew that in his invocation of the ancient powers of Callanish, and in his terrible promise, he had done right. Though what those powers were that made him think and say such things, he did not know or understand. For what power was it that gave eagles power to fly across the sky, and then confined them to a cage? And he wondered where the power came from, and why he trusted it.

4

That same night, at that same moment, and less than a mile from the Zoo, one other living creature was thinking of Minch. It was the Sweeper, whose name was Helmut Wolski.

He had a particular reason for regarding the old female golden eagle as special and, like Creggan, he was obsessed by it now, and stood in his pyjamas staring out of an open window on to a cold and moonlit night. The street below was in darkness but the houses opposite caught the moon's light in their tiles and curtained windows and their shine cast it back upon his troubled face.

The light was not on in his room behind him, and from outside Mr Wolski might have seemed no more than an insubstantial shape, the reds and blues of his pyjamas now turned into grim black stripes against white, such as some of the prisoners in Nazi death camps of the Second World War had worn. He had, for a time, worn such a uniform himself.

He was a short and stocky man who, in different circumstances might have been jocular and tubby, with a wife and grown children, with family photographs on a mantelpiece and the smell of good food in the kitchen. And outside this family home he might have heard the call of the greylag geese as they rose and circled in flight above the River Vistula within whose rolling sight he had been born in 1920.

But it was all gone. The grandmother who had held him for a family photograph; the mother Eda, the father Meir, the brothers Chaim, Avram, Aizik and Josef; the sisters Selma and Esther. Each one of them exterminated in Sobibor, the photograph fluttering into a pile of a thousand personal papers and documents with tens of thousands of spectacles and hundreds of thousands of shoes and boots – to be salvaged or burnt and either way lost for ever.

Wolski survived because his brother Avram put a hand to his back and despite his father's protests pushed him forward from the line when the Germans said they wanted shoemakers and tailors. 'Say you're a tailor,' whispered Avram, and they were the last words any member of his family was ever able to speak to him. He did and as he had some slight training in it he survived in one of the camps that after the war no one remembered.

Sobibor was the scene of the biggest prison escape of the Second World War when six hundred Jews rose against their guards to try to escape to the surrounding forest. These were the Jews who helped maintain the camp and who, like Wolski, had by luck and chance avoided the death that fell upon the majority of the 250,000 Jews who came to Sobibor. Wolski was one of the fifty or so who survived the escape and the remaining months of the war and by a succession of chances so slight, so unpredictable, so arbitrary that they would banish from his mind for ever the belief that there was any sense or pattern to this life, he found his way to Britain in 1945.

Helmut Wolski? No, not his name at all. But the one a British officer in a hurry put to a piece of paper to get Wolski on to his staff, because Wolski had commandeered a horse and the British army needed of all things at that moment a working horse and its apparent owner. Whatever name the frightened young Pole spoke it did not make sense and when a sergeant said, 'It sounds like Wolski, sir,' and smiled, Wolski took the cue and smiled back and nodded, patting the horse and looking positive. The horse would only behave with Wolski and Wolski stayed.

It was in this way that 'Helmut Wolski' found his way to the British, and through them to Britain and, once in London where jobs were scarce, to a job through an army friend at

London Zoo, his family, his past, his very name all gone. And all that was left was a silent man who was imprisoned still by a numbness born of horror and years of fear, tormented by the simple question to which there seemed to be no answer: why, through all the hell he had seen, had *he* survived? And worst of all, he carried with him the sense that he had no right to life, no more than hundreds or thousands of others, starting with his family, who had not lived. So he was a prisoner still, and in this alien world, circumscribed by a tiny room and a job in a Zoo, he had no real friends. To most who knew him he was 'Mr Wolski', who worked hard and rarely spoke.

So Wolski lived alone in a tiny lodging. It was obsessively tidy. There were no pictures on the walls, no ornaments. Just a clock, a small black-and-white television, a few books – an English bible, an atlas, some cheap novels bought second-hand in Camden Town market. His clothes, such as they were, hung in a small wardrobe which, despite its narrowness, was half empty.

There were no signs anywhere of Wolski's background, of the fact that he spoke Polish or had once been Jewish, or of the God that had been present at his birth but on whom he had turned his back before the godlessness in a death camp called Sobibor.

There was a small refrigerator which stuttered and hummed in the night, and some kitchen things. But even allowing for those one strong young man could have come up the stairs to Wolski's room and in a few minutes and one journey have stripped that soulless place of all evidence that for almost three decades, since 1946, Wolski had lived there.

Now, on that strange night, the still figure of Wolski was standing by the window. He was thinking – and something had happened that day to make him do so – about the first time he had seen the female golden eagle in the Zoo. It had been the day he had gone to see about a job he had heard of for a general handyman who had some experience with animals. He had a note from an officer in the army saying that he 'had experience with animals and was reliable'.

That day, while being shown round the Zoo by the Foreman, he came to the Cages just as a female golden eagle was being put in one of them.

'That's our newest arrival,' said the Foreman with a laugh; adding thoughtlessly, 'and I'll bet her conditions are better than the ones you had to put up with in the war. Eh, Mr Wolski?' Mr Wolski did not understand this, but he always smiled when someone in authority smiled and he smiled now. 'What they do to this bird?' he had asked in his still broken English.

'They're putting her in a cage so that people can see her. National institution the Zoo you know, people love to bring the kiddies here and show them all the animals. They like to see a golden eagle, it being the only eagle that lives in Britain.

'This particular bird's just come to the Zoo. The Keeper told me she's come all the way from the Western Isles of Scotland. Lovely place they say, but we go no further north than Southend for our holiday.

'As you can see she's not a juvenile and we only got her because she was caught in a trap set by one of the sheep farmers and broke a wing. Someone found her before the farmer did and so she survived. But she would never fly again, I don't suppose, and anyway we're short of a golden eagle. So it has worked out very well all round.'

Mr Wolski stood by the cage not understanding much of this. All he could see was a proud and fierce eagle, caged in an area that seemed too small for her, and her eyes staring at him blankly. It was a stare he felt he understood, for it felt like his own.

At his lunch break a few days later Mr Wolski took his sandwiches and sat on the benches opposite the eagle and looked at her. Thinking about the bars and wire mesh of her cage, and of how long she would have to be there, he nearly gave up the job there and then. There had been a long time when he had been surrounded by wire and bars. He knew what they were like. He did not like the Zoo anyway. Cages, nets, animals in captivity, humans who were pushed lower than animals – he had seen enough of that.

But jobs were hard to find and he decided not to resign then but to wait a few weeks until he found another job. A few weeks . . . but how soon they turn to months; how soon to years. A whole life may be wasted idling today's minutes in reveries of tomorrow's dreams, until hopes fade and young days have turned into old age.

The Zoo had helped Mr Wolski find rooms nearby and he had made one or two friends among other immigrant Poles. But most of them could not understand his lasting despair, for was he not free and in the very home of democracy? Yes he was free, he would try to explain, free in body but not in spirit, and he found in time that really he preferred to work with animals rather than people. So he stuck with his job at the Zoo.

The Zoo authorities soon recognized that he understood animals and offered to promote him to be one of the keepers. He agreed, on a strange condition: that he would never have to work with the eagles. Which the authorities could not understand, because everyone knew that at lunchtime Mr Wolski always went down to the benches by the Cages and ate his sandwiches looking at the eagles.

The Fifties, the Sixties, decades passed. But the spiritual numbness remained. An armoured glove filled with a sadist's hand had reached into his heart and torn out his joy in life and put in its place a seemingly permanent sense of loss and despair. He survived but had forgotten how to live. His smiles were mirthless, his eyes stared out from behind bars far stronger, far more treacherous, than the real bars and mesh of the Cages.

But a day had come in the Sixties when he was in one of the elephant houses and was staring up at an elephant as it walked neurotically round and round its tiny area when a sudden memory of some of the places he had been kept in during the war had come to him; no space, no freedom, no life. At Sobibor he had not cried out, nor flinched, before the horror and the death he saw. Now, suddenly and violently and ridiculously, he did so. He swung the metal bucket he was carrying in an arc and crashed it against a wall and he stood shaking with horror at himself.

Then the world seemed to be going round and he was falling down and someone was running from a distance, one of the Keepers, in a grey uniform and with a fat pale face that filled him with such fear that he began to cry out in Hebrew words that he had forgotten he knew. It was the Kaddish, part of the daily ritual in the synagogue of which he was no longer a part – a prayer of universal peace, which is especially recited by orphan mourners. Three decades late he spoke it for his parents and his siblings, thinking that the kindly keeper who bent over him was perhaps, after all, SS Sergeant Gustav Wagner, or SS Sergeant Karl Frenzel or . . .

The doctor said he needed a rest and he was away ill for three months. When he came back and saw the cages and animal houses he knew immediately that he would never be able to go inside one of them again. Not even for a second. He needed space around him. Space and air and the chance to go at his own pace, and most of all he needed to get away from the Zoo to that place which in the weeks he had been ill he had begun to sense must exist, though he knew neither its name nor where it might be. Wolski's defences had crumbled and what some might have called a breakdown was the beginning of his recovery to the kindly determined man, or nearly man, he had been before Sobibor. These things he barely understood, and lacking anybody to talk to, it was at lunchtime sitting before an eagle whose name he did not know was Minch that he began to see his way towards them.

His first step towards that freedom was to tell the Zoo authorities that he could not work inside any of the cages or buildings or go where animals were confined. But when he said so, hoping that they would find him a job away from the

Zoo, they said instead that if he wanted he could work through the remaining years to his retirement as general helper and sweeper. It was the same job he had started with at the Zoo so many years before.

Strangely, it was a job that satisfied him, for he did it at his own pace and in his own way, and provided he did it well, which he did, then there was nobody to disturb him. So he swept the paths and repaired the fences and at lunchtime most days would go and sit by himself on the benches, watching the people watching the animals, and sometimes looking at his old friend the golden eagle, who was growing old with him.

Now Mr Wolski shivered as the moon went behind a cloud for a moment leaving just the stars in the night sky. He knew very well that *this* night was the one which would decide whether the old female eagle survived.

For that evening, as work finished, the Zoo Curator himself had summoned him to the building near the Cages where they did a lot of the scientific and veterinary work on the birds. Mr Wolski knew already that the old eagle had been ailing for months now and that three weeks ago they had finally taken her out of her cage and into the veterinary block to see if there was anything they could do for her. The truth was, they regarded her survival after three weeks in care as a miracle.

Yet for a time she had even got better, but then suddenly today – 'or yesterday now' he thought, looking at the luminous dials of the old clock he kept by his bed – she had got worse again. The Curator knew about old Wolski's love of the bird and had called him in.

Then, for the first time in three decades, Mr Wolski had reached out his hands and touched the eagle he had loved and who had given him such comfort for so long. Her great wings were lank and dull, her eyes barely open, and her talons so weak that it was possible to bend them back and forth unresisted. And this eagle had never been one of the easy ones. There had always been such spirit in her.

'The Keeper's for putting her out of her misery now, Mr Wolski and from a scientific point of view I'm inclined to agree with him. He knows these eagles very well and it is possible she is in pain . . . Eh, Mr Wolski?'

Mr Wolski's old head bent over Minch and his hands rested gently on her back. She was not lying down, but rather squatted quietly in the small portable cage into which they had put her. He heard the words the Curator was saying but he made no reply. He knew exactly why the Curator had asked him in to see the eagle – a most unusual thing for someone as unimportant as him to be called in personally in this way. But everyone in the Zoo knew of his love for this particular eagle though all through the years he had resolutely refused ever to handle her.

But now Mr Wolski had been asked to see her, and it was because the Curator, in his kind but mistaken way, thought he might like to take leave of the old eagle. Mr Wolski took his hands from Minch and quietly closed the door of the cage she was in. He kept his head a little bent and did not really look up at the Curator. Indeed, Mr Wolski rarely looked anyone full in the face, seeming meek and quiet as if in a strong wind he might almost have been blown away. But only a strong will had allowed Mr Wolski to survive Sobibor, and the Curator sensed it now.

'I do not think,' said Mr Wolski quietly, 'that any man has the right to take life. When he thinks he has he is at his most dangerous.'

Then he looked at the old eagle again and shaking his head said, 'During the last war when I was a prisoner I knew men who were nearer to death than this and yet by some force of will or perhaps some power greater than us they survived. Or perhaps after all you think it is just chance?' Then he looked at the Curator, straight into his eyes to make him understand that the person he was thinking of was himself. He had stared death in the face and wanted the old eagle to have a chance as he had had. He smiled gently.

'Life is a *wonderful* thing, Curator, and its pulse beats still in the heart of my old friend here. Perhaps it is best to leave it there for a little longer.'

Then he had gone, and the Curator had stared for a long time after him, and then at the golden eagle who stared blankly back at him.

'Well, I don't know,' he said to himself. 'Maybe the Keeper's right, maybe Mr Wolski's right. On the whole I think she can struggle on just a bit longer . . .'

After his conversation with the Zoo Curator Mr Wolski had gone down to the eagles and stared into Minch's empty cage. Then he looked up at the new young golden eagle who had been available under special government licence and brought in as her replacement. He had been the weaker of a hatching of two males and would almost certainly have died within a few days if local ornithologists had not taken him from the nest and reared him themselves in the hope that a home might finally be found for him as worthwhile as the Zoo . . .

That he was still a juvenile was evident from the lighter markings on his wings that are lost only in maturity. The eagle stared back at him proudly and without fear and Mr Wolski wondered how long he would be here in captivity, staring out at the same things year after year, his great wings never feeling the power and support of the wind, his talons never arcing forward and down as they did what they had been made for and struck at prey.

Mr Wolski was suddenly angry at the Zoo for keeping such creatures in such a way. Angry and . . .

. . . and now, hours later, deep into the night Mr Wolski felt that anger still. But he felt as well something far greater – the sudden joy of life that he had pleaded for as the old eagle's right, and in pleading for it then had begun at last to claim it as his own. He breathed deeply, and lacking anything better to do opened his bedroom window even further and leaned out into the cold night. Clouds drifted across the sky and revealed the moon again.

From far off where the Zoo lay the howl of a lone wolf wound up into the night. And then another, soft and sorrowful above the houses of north-west London but then on into the free night.

Mr Wolski thought of his friend the eagle who was struggling for life through this long night. Then he did something he had not done for years, for decades, since before the darkness came to his own life in the Second World War: he said a silent prayer. Not to a Jewish God, not to a Christian one, not in Hebrew or English but in his native Polish, and to whatever power it was that made the stars shine, and the clouds drift, a lone wolf howl, and an eagle fly free over wild country.

'Let her be free,' he whispered, 'let her go free.' And then he did something else he had not done for decades, in fact since he was a boy in his beloved Poland. He made a bargain with the power he had invoked. 'The day she is free then I will leave the Zoo and never return, whatever hardship it may involve. I will never go back.' And he knew that she might be free this very night, free to fly where no man could cage her. He knew that if he had had the courage he would have vowed then and there never to go back, but such courage was not his yet, but was it so bad for a man who could make no sense of how he had come to be where he was to rest his fate on the unknown course of an eagle's life?

Mr Wolski turned back to his bed content to have made a decision by which he would stand, and feeling that the tiredness he felt coming over him was decades old. Before he finally lay down to rest and sleep he hesitated over whether to cross his small room again and close the window on the chilly night. But with a shake of his head and a gentle smile he decided against doing so, for he liked the feeling of freedom the open window gave him.

*

While less than a mile away, as the moon came out again from behind clouds, it shone through a window into a cage where an old eagle perched and its light fell across her head and one of her wings. It seemed to fill her plumage with its cold light as her body shivered for a moment, her head trembled and her eyes, which had been half closed, slowly opened. She stared out of the window and saw the stars and a bright moon. And near by she heard the howling of the wolves.

For a moment that might have lasted hours she seemed to see herself, old and weak, and knew that now she could be free and the burden of life leave her wings for ever. But from somewhere she heard a calling that whispered the sacred word 'Callanish' and said that no Callanish eagle could die here so far from home where no eagle ever flew.

'And anyway,' whispered another voice, and one that was rather more matter-of-fact because it was her own, 'there's a young eagle out there called Creggan who needs to know a few things if he's going to survive and be free.'

Then Minch fluttered her wings, and scuffled her talons, and pulled her head a little higher to make herself look as proud in the darkness as she felt. For she was a Callanish eagle and was going to teach that eagle from Wrath just what that meant before she allowed herself to fade away into darkness . . .

5

The first sign to Creggan that something to do with Minch might be happening came at last nearly four weeks later when the Men opened up her cage again. They entered and sprayed it out with water. Then they brought food in and laid it inside her shelter.

'There you are,' said Kraal miserably, 'I told you there was no hope. They've got another eagle coming and they're preparing a cage for him.'

But Creggan was not so sure. He had taken stance near one side of Minch's cage and was waiting, hardly daring to look to see if Minch was coming, or to think of it; or even to hope.

It was a lovely summer's morning and as a light breeze ruffled the leaves of the trees on the Three Island Pond enclosure everything was warm and slow. There was a fine blue sky with great white clouds in the distance, and even the restless tiger had stopped still and was dozing, his great eyes staring out peacefully on the world as he occasionally licked a paw and groomed himself.

Creggan suddenly felt strength and great certainty. He turned to Kraal and said, 'These preparations are for Minch's return. You will soon see that I have been right all this time. She will come back.'

But Kraal only shook his head and stared mournfully out on to the lovely morning, seeing only a memory of an old eagle he had argued with but always loved and who would never come back.

The Men left the cage, closed the gate again, and walked

away. As the morning progressed the Zoo began to fill up with visitors and the sound of children's laughter.

The day passed slowly into afternoon. The tiger stood up and stretched and began his pacing again, back and forth, on and on.

Creggan stayed where he had been in the morning, firm and sure. He stared steadily outwards towards the ducks and flamingos while Kraal mantled his plumage, let out a harsh call or two and dropped down into the shelter to pick at the remnant of meat he had left over from the previous day. Gradually the sun fell away behind the trees on Three Island Pond whose shadows slowly lengthened towards the Cages.

'It's no good thinking she's going to come because she's not,' called out Kraal from his shelter between bites at his new food. 'And anyway . . .'

But Creggan was not listening, for a strange thing had happened.

Slorne, who had been up at the back of her cage most of the day as usual, suddenly opened her wings, swung round and dropped down to the front of her cage. She jerked her head round quickly towards where the Men usually came from and stared fixedly. Creggan had never seen her at the front of her cage before. Her talons grasped the mesh of the cage, her beak strained at the front as if she knew that something important was happening. Then Creggan saw in the distance two of the Men coming, the Keeper and one other.

The Keeper was carrying a portable cage and from it peered an eagle. An old eagle. A female eagle. A golden eagle!

'It's Minch,' whispered Creggan. And then more loudly, 'It's Minch!'

And then he let out a call of welcome and triumph and he turned round in his cage and, raising his wings, flew up and dashed his talons against the very top of his cage and, wheeling sideways, hit against the side of Minch's cage as well so that the Cages were filled with the sound of his joy.

As Minch was carried past Woil's cage he said, 'Nice Men

brought Minch back to us. Minch was good, so kind Men brought her back. See, Kraal,' he called out in his silky voice, 'bold Creggan was right and you too will be pleased at Man's good nature . . .'

Kraal could hardly believe his eyes as the Keeper carried Minch into the cage, and just stared in amazement, for once saying nothing at all. Instead he looked through the cages towards Woil and with one fierce look stopped his babbling short.

The Keeper waited while the other Man closed the door behind him and then set the cage on the ground and let Minch free. She hopped clear and opened her wings and in one sudden jump was up on the bare branch. The Keeper picked up the cage and backed out, his helper careful to close the gate quickly behind him as he came out.

Even at such a moment as that there were eagles in other parts of the Cages who seemed not to have noticed what had happened. They continued to feed, or stared out on the Zoo not looking in the direction of Minch at all; while Creggan was so busy staring at Minch in delight and pleasure that he did not notice behind him, in the next-door cage, Slorne stare for the moment at Minch and then swing round and silently resume her vigil at the back top of her cage, looking at the trees and sky.

'Are you all right, Minch, really all right?' asked Kraal the moment the Men had gone.

'I am still a little weak,' said Minch, 'but there is nothing wrong now that won't mend soon enough.'

'I *said* you'd come back,' said Creggan. 'I told him you were a Callanish eagle and would not die here.'

'I know,' said Minch softly, 'I felt your strength in my weakest hour. Your faith gave me new life and strength. But I fear you may live to regret it, Creggan.'

Creggan was startled by this and wondered if in some way she understood that he had made a vow that if ever the chance came for them to escape he would place her freedom before his own.

'The months ahead are going to be hard, for during them I am going to put you through much learning and discipline,' said Minch speaking in a strong and determined way. 'There is not much time left now for I will not always be here to help you and you must learn from me what you can. You may not like me for it but I will have to drive you hard if you are to learn all you will need to survive what you will face. What we all face.'

Creggan looked at her and then, mantling his wings, glared angrily at the world outside the Cages, a glare that took in the Zoo, the Men, the trees, the wind and even the sky, and said loudly, 'I can face anything, anything!'

'Creggan, do not waste your energy fighting the wind or the world! The enemy I speak of is there in your cage with you.'

Creggan immediately turned round as if expecting to see some mighty enemy near by. He raised his wings and clattered about his cage, dashing his talons and beak against the bars and wire mesh to make as much noise as possible. Then he dived down to the pool of water at the front of his cage and splashed it here and there.

After a few minutes of this he grew breathless with anger and rage and flurried his wings so much that he was hardly able to lift them any more he was so tired.

Kraal laughed at him.

'I said you didn't understand much, Creggan,' he reminded him, 'when Minch was ill. She is talking about an enemy which you cannot see or hear or smell.'

Creggan bowed his head. He felt foolish.

'I don't understand,' he said.

'Here we are very safe,' said Minch, 'and we cannot be hurt. Our food is brought to us, and so we never hunt or seek prey. Some of us, including yourself, Creggan, came here before they had ever learnt to hunt, or even to fly. We have forgotten how to read the winds or easily find directions from the stars; we do not know any more how to read the landscape, and you, Creggan, cannot recognize friend from enemy among our own kind. I am the only golden eagle you know now and you may think all are like me, and become trusting and believe they will help you. But many will be your enemies, many will try even to fight you.

'Being here in perpetual safety we forget how hard the world is outside and how strong and determined we must be if ever we want to live in it again. The enemy that Kraal was trying to describe is really yourself, Creggan. For a part of you will not want to fight or learn or struggle. That part of you is very cunning and it will slowly fight with the other part that yearns for freedom and true strength. It will not fight by raising its wings and clashing its talons and making noise; but quietly, cleverly, making you see the Men as friends, making you fear the wide world outside, so that when opportunity comes you will not take it as you should but hide behind excuses like 'The time isn't right yet' or 'I don't think I can do *that*'. Until the time will come when that enemy in you will win and your yearning for freedom will be only a lie which you turn into dreams that start 'if only . . .' If onlys are things that eagles prefer to talk about than do. Do you understand what I am saying, Creggan?'

Creggan nodded.

'Do you really understand?'

Creggan was silent. For an eagle who had been so ill Minch was doing a good job being terrifying. He did not know what to think, or what to say. She made it sound so complicated. All he wanted was to be free. To be able to fly. To see her free. If only the cage was not there . . . If only! He had spoken it already.

'I will try to learn to understand,' he said.

'You will grow to hate me, I'm afraid,' said Minch matter-of-factly. 'But I'm afraid there's no helping that.' Then she turned to speak to all the eagles there, for most were listening

in silence to her except those, and there were some, who had
been so long in the Cages or so affected by them that they
showed interest in nothing but food, their spirit killed by
imprisonment.

'You others will tell Creggan what you know and can
remember and in telling him will remind yourselves of what
you may have forgotten. I am certain that in time and with
courage one of us will leave this place but we must always
remember that our first enemy is ourselves. Opportunity will
come and in teaching the youngest of us to prepare for it we
will all of us be fitter to take it should it come our way.'

The more Minch had said the quieter Kraal had become.
He remembered how Minch had spoken to him like this
when he had first come to the Cages. And how in the months
and years ahead he had grown angry with her, for she would
never let him forget that he was caged and unfree. She always
wanted him to tell her where he came from because she said,
as she had said to Creggan on his first night, that for an eagle
to survive the first thing he must know is where he comes
from, and he must not forget his memories however distant
they may be. They make up his hope and give him his
strength. Then Kraal remembered that when Creggan had
asked him about where he came from all he had said was 'the
South' and not really told him any more. He had wanted to
forget . . . just as Minch had told him he would.

Well, he could remember, and he wasn't afraid, for he could
remember even now . . . and Kraal began to speak: 'You asked
me where I came from, Creggan, and I will tell you. There
was a great lake and on it were flamingos like the ones you
see every day on Three Island Pond. Thousands of them, and
more than that. They stretched in great flocks wider than the
whole of the Zoo. And the colours of the sky above them in
the evening were ever-changing blues, greys and pinks so
that the flamingos seemed reflections of it sometimes. Then
they would suddenly all rise up as one, their great wings
sweeping them rhythmically over the water, their legs

stretched behind them, thousands of them flying above that great lake.

'We had a nest of white sticks in a tree and I can remember others of our kind soaring high on the wind and then stooping from out of that same hot sky, down towards the surface of the lake, their stoop so fast that you could hear the winds riffling and racing in their outstretched wings. Then they would bring their talons forward and reach their beaks out and in one swift movement crash them on the surface of the still lake, and out of the splashing spray caused by their wings as they beat to gain height again they would rise struggling with a fish in their talons.'

'I can remember the red deer on the hills below our homesite,' whispered Creggan in reply, his gaze passing out through the cage to the warm evening beyond, 'as they came grazing in herds along the distant glen. There was a lake there but not big like the one you knew, Kraal. It was small and murky and we called it a lochan. But by its side the red deer would stop and drink and . . .' And as he and Kraal continued to talk old Minch quietly dropped down to her shelter and took up the food there, listening to their few memories of the world outside.

She was glad to be back, glad she had survived and felt now that she had a purpose she had not had before. She would teach Creggan the eagle lore she knew, and remind Kraal of what he had perhaps begun to forget. But she knew it would be hard and that the time would surely come when Creggan would grow angry with her as Kraal had done. But she also knew that anger would be part of Creggan's survival, part of the strength he would need if, as she hoped, his chance for freedom ever came. If it did it might only be for a moment, the briefest of seconds, and she wanted Creggan to be ready for it. For if only he could fly free then perhaps this life of hers would not have been in vain.

As Creggan and Kraal continued to tell their dearest memories, night began to fall and Minch began to plan out what she would do in the limited time she felt she had left to her. Her wings might be old and her talons blunt but strangely her illness had sharpened her mind even more and she knew that somehow a chance would come. Suddenly. Unexpectedly. And she wanted Creggan, who was youngest among them, to be ready to take it.

6

Once the eagles had got used to the return of Minch they settled down for the summer months.

During the day there were so many people visiting the Zoo that there was no chance for Minch to teach those things she thought Creggan should know. So she did it in the early morning before the Men came, or in the warm evenings when the Zoo gates were shut.

Then Minch would talk quietly to Creggan and speak of the lore of golden eagles which his parents had begun to tell him.

'Our kind is the greatest of the birds that fly in this land,' she explained. 'And although we now occupy only one part of it, the northern and oldest part, yet once our range was wider. But Men persecuted us and other birds of prey like us were poisoned, trapped and shot. Our numbers declined.

'Some, like the osprey and the peregrine falcon, which flies even more swiftly than we do, almost died out. Others, like the kestrels, learned to live with Man and others learned like us to avoid him. We made our place the upper glens and moorlands of Scotland in the north where Men could less easily find us. We chose sites that were obscure and hard to see from the valleys, at the base of upland cliffs from where we could see but not be seen. There is great skill in choosing a site and this must I teach you, though it is long since I made a site.'

'How long?' asked Creggan, for he loved to hear Minch talk of her past life. 'How long have you been here?'

'It is thirty years now, perhaps a few more. I came at the same time as the Sweeper came for I saw him standing by this very cage in clothes the people wear and not in Keeper-clothes such as he began to wear afterwards.'

'How were you caught?'

'It was chance and yet I blame myself. On the Callanish moorland there are not many features, except for one thing I will tell you about soon. But there was a post on the lonely road and sometimes if I was tired from hunting I would take stance on it for a few moments, to rest. A good place, for you could see danger or prey for miles.

'But not good enough. A Man must have seen me take stance there regularly and known I might come back again. It was a wet and stormy day, which grew dark while I was still far from my site. I had caught an eider duck that had been sheltering on a lochan and was flying back with it against the wind when I grew tired.

'Ahead I saw the post on the road, but it was dark and murky with wind and rain in my face. As I approached it I reached out my talons to land and perhaps the prey I was holding obscured the view for I should have seen sooner what had been put on top of the post by Men. It was a metal trap. Even as I put my talons down I pulled them away, for I sensed something was wrong, but it was quicker than I and with a loud metal sound like the closing of a cage gate it sprang shut.

'It did not catch my foot, for I was already wheeling away, but it crashed down on my wing and caught it in its grip. With the sudden pain darkness came over me . . . I must have been unconscious for hours. When I came out of a nightmare of pain it was to a swirling world of night, and a storm. I was hanging from my wing down the length of the pole, the wind strong enough to pull and toss my body against it, and each time it did the pain at my wing was so terrible that I cried out. There was continuous driving rain, and a cold that numbed me. I knew then that my last hours had come but was in such agony that I began to wish they would come sooner. Yet worse was to follow!'

The Cages had fallen silent as Minch told her story, for it was many years since she had recounted it and then only briefly. There was anger among them, and pity, for each in their different way had seen suffering and did not wish to see it again. Each had something to fear from Men, though Men now protected them in the Cages.

'Somehow I survived that long cold night and in the morning the wind stilled and a chill grey mist drifted over the moors. It is unlike anything you will ever see here, Creggan. It slinks greyly among the marram grass; it slides over and under barbed wire; it makes an eagle lose direction and settles a dank wetness on his feathers; it softens the landscape into obscurity, it hides the familiar cliffs, it turns sheep into monsters and highland cattle into roaring mountains which lurch up towards an eagle out of the clinging mist.

'Such a mist came that grim morning and with it a sound I feared then and fear now. The harsh cruel calls of hooded crows. They are different from the crows that caw in the trees above our Cages here in the south for their feathers are partly grey and in a moorland mist they seem bigger. Where one is, others soon will be. When one finds defenceless prey, others will soon come. They are the eagles' oldest foe and because they are clever and know they cannot fight us by themselves they will mob us with numbers, and try to make us drop our prey.

'Their beaks are sharp and know where to find the vulnerable parts of a prey's body: belly, throat and eyes.'

Creggan shuddered, for without eyes an eagle is nothing.

'I heard them scavenging along the road somewhere in the mist. It was a good place to find carrion because cars used that road occasionally and no doubt caught voles and such creatures in their wheels.

'I could hear their croaking and their arguments and they came ever nearer until suddenly out of the mist I saw the grey shadow of a wing and wet spike of a beak. It disappeared

again but another came in view and there was a clatter of
wings as two landed on the road twenty feet from where I
hung. I stayed still, hoping desperately that they would not
see me, for I knew that if they did they would lose no time in
tormenting me and finally killing me. A third hooded crow
joined them. They pecked at some dead creature on the
moorland verge, squabbling over which of them should have
it, wheeling and darting at each other like terrible shadows
in the mist. My free wing hung from the pole for I could not
easily close it without terrible pain; my eyes were fixed on
them. My talons ready to do battle as best I could.

'But I knew in my heart that I would have no chance
against them and that they would be merciless. The wind
and the mist whispered in the grass at the foot of the pole
from which I hung. A sheep walked down the road seeming
big in the swirling grey white.

' "It will frighten them away," I thought.

'But the opposite happened. They heard it, wheeled up in
the air towards it and right past me and it turned off the road
in fear. Then, coming back, one of them saw me, or perhaps
my loose wing.

'He slowed in flight, rolled expertly, backed away and then
stalled and hung on the thin wind all at once. Staring. I have
never seen such a terrible run of expressions in a pair of eyes.
Curiosity, surprise, fear, pleasure and finally cruelty.

' "Well, look what we have here!" he said, his voice as cold
and sharp as ice hanging from rock.

' "What is it? We want to see; we'll take, we'll have, we'll
kill, we want!" the other two cried.

'They flocked around the pole, not daring immediately to
come too near, their eyes and beaks devouring my body as I
watched.

' "She is an eagle!" said one with pleasure.

' "A very vulnerable eagle," said another.

' "An eagle that would be better dead," said the third.

' "We'll have, we'll take, we'll stab and pierce . . ." their

voices were the sounds of which nightmares are made. I tried
to lunge at them with my talons but crows are clever, crows
can judge distance to the fraction of a talon.

' "She cannot move!" said one.

' "Not much at least," said another.

' "Certainly not . . . to catch me here!" said the third, lifting
on the breeze above me and hovering over the top of the pole
where the trap was. He landed and stared down at me and at
the blood of my broken wing, his terrible beak opening just
a little with the pleasure of what he saw; while I hung there,
trying to watch all three at once and knowing that one of
them would attack suddenly and then be gone as another
came in from a different direction. I knew that there is no
death worse for an eagle than death at the beaks of hooded
crows. Mean, cruel, vicious and nasty. To blind a lamb or
blind an eagle; all the same to them if it left them with
defenceless prey to kill.

'But they are cowards at heart and hang back until they are
sure they are safe, even then leaving themselves a route for
escape. First to come, first to flee, that's the crow. I felt a
stabbing pain in my caught wing as the one on the top of the
pole lunged with his beak at where he saw blood.

' "Very good, very, very nice," he gloated.

'Then one of the others grew bolder and flew straight at my
face. I raised my free wing and nearly caught him with it and
he called out in alarm. But then the other came at me, and the
one on the top stabbed again, and I knew that now there
were moments only. I twisted on the pole, pushed my talons
forward and caught one of them a passing blow. But he fell
away again unhurt as one of the others dived forward at my
eyes. I tried to stab my beak at them, to catch them with my
talons, to use what strength was left in my wing, but the pain
of it all was terrible and I was weakening with each second
that passed by and before each new attack. And sometimes
since I have wished . . .' and here Minch dropped her voice
low as if she was ashamed of what she was about to say,

'. . . . well, there have been times when it seemed it might have been better if they had taken me. A moment's pain then might have avoided a lifetime of imprisonment since. So easily, Creggan, may an eagle give way to weakness.

'It is easy here, where we are safe from danger, to imagine ourselves out there being strong and doing all sorts of brave and clever things. It is a very different thing when you are out there in the real world beyond the Cages! That is why it is so important that you learn from me all that you can.'

But Creggan was not interested right then in learning, all he wanted to know was what happened next when Minch had been hanging from the pole trap.

'I knew there were only seconds to go and could feel my strength failing with each moment, and a drifting kind of sleep coming on me which whispered, "Give up, Minch, give up . . ." and it was only the knowledge that I was of Callanish, the greatest of the sites, that kept me fighting those few more seconds. Raising my talons just one more time, and one more time after that. Using my beak as best I could, fending them off with my free wing. Seconds . . . but seconds that saved my life.

'For all at once there was a rumble and a roaring along the road in the mist, and the hooded crows rose up in alarm at the sound of it. As they did so there came out of the mist a car and it must have seen the crows at me for it stopped. I knew then that my end had come for surely it was the Man who had put the trap on the pole to catch me. The crows skulked away into the mist, chattering among themselves that they would be back when the Man had gone, and I hung there helpless. Yet, strangely, even as he approached I could tell he would not harm me. He had the same feeling about him as the Sweeper has, as some creatures have, like Slorne over there. You know that such a one will never harm you.'

Creggan nodded silently, his eyes wide. He understood what she meant about Slorne because as the days and weeks had grown into months he had found great comfort in her strange and silent presence. He knew very well that she meant only good.

'So it was with this Man,' continued Minch. 'He gently lifted my body up to take the weight off my wing and then freed me from the trap. He placed me on the ground and saw at once that I could not fly. He wrapped me in a warm coat and placing me in the car took me several miles over the moor. Although I was in pain I was conscious and can remember seeing Callanish itself. How strange it looked from below! I saw it as Men must see it and not as an eagle does.'

'You saw what?' asked Creggan.

'Have I not told you of Callanish?' Minch sounded vague, her voice seeming to come from a distance . . . 'It is important to know of it if you are to understand our lore, though I think you already know more of it then you realize . . . But I must first finish the tale of how I came to be here.

'We came to a lonely place where I could hear the sea crashing on rocks near by. It was a house, warm and comfortable. There were cages too for animals, but different from the ones here. Simple and quite open, temporary cages. There was a seal there in some water, a great herring gull with a damaged foot, and other creatures. All were injured in some way like me.

'He put me out in a field inside a small enclosure. There was a wire mesh roof over it lower than in the Cages and some fish and meat. Every morning and evening he came and my wing got better, though it still hurt and was just a little crooked.

'The days grew warm and I began to hop around the cage and try to fly again. But it was hard, very hard, and my wing was still weak. Then a day came when he took me outside. There was another Man there but not so nice. He had a roughness about him. They watched me trying to fly but I could not. My wing was crooked. I knew I needed time to learn to fly again. Then one day they took me out again and let me free to try to fly for myself, and I knew that I must try, for much depended on it. So I did, and I managed to rise a little way, but my wing hurt and the sea wind tugged at it and below me there suddenly flew some hooded crows and I was afraid and panicked, and nearly fell from the sky. The Men came for me where I huddled in the marram grass and they took me back to the low cage.

'Soon after that a different Man came by car and he put me in a carrier cage and took me into the darkness of a long journey, over bumpy roads, on to a ship, and into the most terrible place of all, an iron cage with obscured windows, which raced through the night clattering and clattering, a regular rhythm of metallic sound. The sound of Man. Hootings and shouts, hot mist and lights . . . and I was numb with fear.

'Then I came here, and here I have been ever since, wondering often if it would have been better if that first Man had never found me.'

Silence fell as Creggan and the other eagles that had been listening thought about what Minch had told them.

'Perhaps,' said Kraal finally, 'it would have been better after all.'

But Minch shook her head. 'There was a night a few weeks past, when I was ill, when my spirit left my body and I wanted to be free for ever. But you see, Kraal, there is always hope, and there are eagles here who may yet learn what I have seen. And anyway, I am of Callanish and though Creggan here does not yet know much of the site of Creggan yet he knows what that means.'

'I'm not sure,' hesitated Creggan, 'I don't really know . . .'

He was thinking that the night Minch had referred to must have been the one when he had made a plea to the powers that rule the skies where eagles fly. He had invoked the name of Callanish and it had sent its power into Minch and left him with a promise he must keep: to put her life before his own if ever chance or opportunity came. And yet, he did not really know what Callanish was.

'All I know of Callanish is the little my parents told me,' said Creggan. 'But I do not know *what* it is, or even what is there! Can you tell me?'

But despite all Creggan's entreaties for her to talk more of Callanish, Minch refused, saying she was tired and must rest. Only when the time felt right would she speak of Callanish.

7

'Nice Men, kind Men, very welcome Men.'

It was Woil greeting the Men on a sunny afternoon in late summer as they started to bring the food along the eagles' cages.

Creggan was doing his best to ignore Woil, who he did not trust or like. He always talked nicely to the Men even though they could not understand a word he said. He made himself as meek as a lamb, hoping perhaps that they would give him an extra morsel of food or some other favour.

'No pride in that buzzard, none at all!' Kraal was inclined to say, fixing Woil with a glare and flexing his talons back and forth to make it clear that it was just as well there were three cages between them because if there weren't . . .

Two of the Men began to open the Cages one by one from the far end as they brought food to each of the eagles. From the other end a party of visitors began their walking stare along the Cages. They were laughing and talking and putting black square things to their faces, pointing them at the eagles, and clicking them.

'It's a ritual,' Minch had once explained. 'The visitors have been doing it as long as I can remember.'

'What's it mean?' asked Creggan.

'Well, they find something to click at and when they've clicked at it they don't look at it any more but move on and click at something else.'

The Men were progressing up towards them and were just about to reach Woil, who, as usual, was swaying back and forth on his stance with a pleasant expression on his face as he intoned, 'Lovely Men, so good to me, so generous to Woil, who is good and never tries to hurt you. Pleasant Men, very, very nice Men . . .'

Creggan was watching the group of people coming along from the other direction and making a lot of noise. Some were eating and there was always the chance when this happened that they might put something into the Cages for the eagles.

Minch had long ago taught Creggan to ignore this altogether as their food was never good and an eagle could only come to harm if he got involved with people in that way.

'Anyway,' she had said, 'the Men don't like it and I've seen them get quite angry with people who do it. People have been attacked by the eagles and in my younger days there was an occasion when I myself attacked a visitor.'

What a lovely day it is, Creggan was thinking to himself, warm and sunny, and the Zoo full of interest, and food on its way with only Woil and Slorne to be fed before it was his turn, and the people were coming very near, *too* near. In fact . . . one of them was stuffing something through the wire and bars of his cage which they shouldn't be doing and he didn't much like it . . . Creggan was staring in a hostile way at this invasion of his territory but feeling too lazy to bother much about it when to his astonishment he heard a familiar and unpleasant voice say something unfamiliar and very strange indeed.

'Attack!' said the voice, 'attack NOW!'

The voice was that of Woil the buzzard who at that same moment was having the door of his cage opened by one of the Men with food.

Creggan looked round in surprise. There was Woil with the usual Man-welcoming expression on his face and looking as harmless as a tired sparrow and saying, 'Nice Man, welcome food, good to bring it to grateful Woil. ATTACK, CREGGAN OF WRATH! NOW IS THE MOMENT I

HAVE WAITED FOR! Good Man, very jolly decent nice Man. NOW, CREGGAN, *NOW!* Extremely nice Man . . .'

There was such urgency in Woil's commands that Creggan did not hesitate. He raised his wings and pulled them back a little, bent his head forward, slightly opened his beak, and lunged forward and down at the white flesh of the hand that was pushing itself with a piece of sandwich through the front bars of his cage. He flew forward as if there were no bars there at all. His talons swung down and ahead of him and opened starkly towards the vulnerable hand.

As they found their target their points tightened into a terrible grip as the rest of his body thumped against the front of the cage. He opened his wings in great noisy sweeps to keep his balance as he gripped on to the hand.

The next few seconds seemed to move so fast that none of the witnesses to it, eagles or people, could ever quite remember the sequence of events. Certainly the visitor whose hand Creggan had so swiftly and accurately caught in his talons let out a cry of alarm and pain, trying to pull his hand away. Certainly the Man who had just opened the door of Woil's cage had his attention distracted by the shout.

But what else happened remains unclear. People surged forward and back; the Man realized he was needed and turned to go out of Woil's cage, probably thinking that if he left the door ajar for only a moment Woil was too placid and safe a bird to try to escape.

Woil's eyes were fixed on that door with the intensity of an eagle stooping on prey. Even as the Man hesitated at the door, one hand across it while he stared in surprise and alarm at the person caught by the young golden eagle, even at that moment Woil dived forward with a speed and aggression that no Man and no eagle would have expected of 'loyal Woil'.

And in a second he was under the Man's arm and out through the cage door, free and gliding over towards the fence by the benches.

Then a silence began to fall on every living thing around

the Cages except for a Man running, not towards Woil but to the visitor caught by the hand in the talons of Creggan. Seeing the Man approach Creggan pulled away and with one final lunge of his beak at the flesh hopped back and up on to the branch across his cage. He stared down at the whimpering person beyond the front of the cage, at the people around, at the Man staring at him for a moment, and then at Woil who had taken stance on a litter bin.

The silence continued to fall. Creggan watched Woil who looked smaller on the litter bin out in the great free world than he had in the cage. Woil looked around him and seemed suddenly confused and unsure of himself. His head kept dipping and his wings half opening as he tried to retain his balance on his awkward stance. Creggan, Minch, Kraal and even Slorne were watching him, each one of them still as ice.

The world of the Zoo seemed to move without any noise at all and around the Cages all was still but for the visitor Creggan had attacked, who swayed back and forth where he sat on the ground, others gathered around him. Then the silence in the Zoo became complete.

Woil stared around him and then suddenly with a push of his wings raised himself into the air, turned, and landed ten feet away on the back of a green bench. Creggan could see that he was afraid and that his fear was making him terribly uncertain.

Slowly, like a black storm cloud that builds up ominously on a distant horizon, the second of the two Men who had been feeding the eagles advanced on Woil. The Man had taken his jacket off and was holding it out in front of him and all of them could see what he intended to do. But Woil did not move away. He stared back at the Cages, he glanced up at the trees behind them, he stared at the people who stared at him. Nothing but the Man moved, and he moved slowly and seemed to get bigger all the time. He spoke softly in a voice very like the one Woil had used: 'Nice bird, pleasant bird, bird come to no harm, Man not hurt this buzzard, Man only want to stop him feeling afraid, Man only want to put him back where he is safe; nice food waiting.'

Creggan could not understand the Man's words but to him they seemed to sound like that. Such wormy words would surely make an eagle back away in fear. But not Woil. He wavered and dithered on the seat, he looked back at his previous stance and then at the Man and then flew back to the litter bin and took stance on it again.

It was full of paper, ice-cream tubs and things that might excite the curiosity of any creature.

'But surely, not *now*!' thought Creggan as, to his astonishment, Woil began to peck and ferret among the rubbish in the bin, ignoring the approaching man altogether.

A hundred yards beyond Woil a pair of white seagulls wheeled round in the sky, dived over Three Island Pond, and then soared up over the Zoo, free against the summer sky. A flock of chattering sparrows came over the Cages, landed on the grass by the litter bin where Woil had taken stance, and then twittered off again over the tigers' cages. The Man reached Woil and with a slow but sure movement put the coat he had been carrying over Woil's back and head and quickly put his arms around him. He then picked him up and in a few moments had taken Woil back to his cage, put him in, closed the iron gate and secured it.

Sounds came back to the watching eagles. People moving, people speaking, children laughing and playing somewhere in the distance. The Man who had scared Creggan off the person he had attacked stared into Creggan's cage for a moment, then at Minch, and then joined the other one. The two Men talked. They carried away the bin of meat fragments they had been carrying. The people dispersed, talking in low voices.

Woil's escape was over, and it had all taken less than a minute and a half.

For a time the eagles were speechless with surprise at what had happened and could only stare through the Cages to Woil who had now taken stance again on the branch where he had originally been and was grooming himself as if nothing had happened.

It was Creggan who impetuously broke the silence.

'Why didn't you try to fly away?' he asked. 'Why didn't you escape? Why did you let the Men catch you again?'

Woil stared round at him and seemed to be in a state of shock. He tried to speak and could not, and then tried again. Eventually he said in a strange and distant voice, 'The sky was so . . . big . . . so daunting . . . and I was afraid. Whichever way I turned looked bigger and wider and further than the other. It was all around me and I did not dare to go in any direction. I was confused, I could not seem to raise my wings. And then seagulls flew free, and a flock of sparrows, and they seemed to own the sky and not me. But for a moment, between the door of the cage and where I first took stance, I could feel the greatness of the sky, it was on my wings. So big, so huge, so frightening. I could not seem to find the courage to fly free. I never understood before that the sky might be frightening.'

Then with his head low and his wings cast disconsolately down, Woil dropped to the floor of the cage, put a talon in the meat that the Man had dropped there when Creggan had made his attack near by, and pulled it back and out of sight in the cage's shelter.

Creggan turned to Minch, who had watched it all as well.

'Why?' was all he could ask. 'If only it had been me I would have flown to the highest tree where they couldn't catch me and then, and then into the sky to find the wind.'

'If only!' said Minch. 'I have warned you of that. Easy to say, Creggan, harder to do. What you have seen today may well be the best lesson you will ever learn of the difficulties facing us in the outside world. Leave Woil for now, for he has need to be by himself. He will tell us more of the fear he felt and we will learn from it.'

'But *Woil*!' said Kraal with just a little admiration in his voice. 'He is the last one here I would have expected to think of doing that.'

'That is what he wanted us all to think, including the Men,' said Minch, 'and we should honour him for his cunning and intelligence. When the moment came he took it and he took it well. With speed and aggression as an *eagle* should.

'Know then that there is a bird of prey here to respect and admire. He has fooled even us with his pleasant talk to the Men all these years. His plan to escape was so long in the making and the lesson for us must lie in the reason why, when the time came, he could not make it work. Listen well when he tells us what happened out there to him and respect him for what he has done, and honour him, for at least he has given each of us hope and proof that escape is possible.'

8

Autumn came suddenly that year. The sun grew golden and weak, dew formed on the grass by the benches in front of the Cages, and great clouds of starlings squealed out of empty evening skies and formed and re-formed and grouped yet again round and over the Zoo.

The nights grew colder, but in the early morning the rising sun was caught a thousand times in the droplets of moisture that formed in the webs that spiders wove across the bars of Creggan's cage.

Watching these changes about him, and seeing the leaves of the trees behind the cages turn rusty brown and then come tumbling down on gusts of wind, Creggan grew restless and ill at ease.

Each of them had been badly affected by Woil's failed escape in the summer and now their sense of captivity was made even worse by the feeling of change, renewal and purpose in the air.

Winter was coming, and eagles wanted to be out there on the winds, planning, checking over territory, grouping after the isolations of spring and summer mating and rearing. Eagles needed to witness the migrations of the smaller birds, or to fly afield to see the world beyond territories which at other times of the year they spent their time protecting and never left. But most of all eagles wanted to see the young take flight, and venture away from their parents and explore the world where they, like the adults, must learn to survive the winter.

Woil himself was much quieter now, and very sad. Gone

was the voice that used to say 'Nice Man, good Man, come to give Woil food!' That had all been an act, partly to lull the Men into trusting him but also, Creggan now realized, to hide the same feelings as they all had in captivity: a game to while away the endless waiting.

Kraal, who had been Woil's greatest mocker and enemy now became his greatest friend, for he admired Woil's cunning and quick thinking, and grieved to see him so downcast. The two would take low stances in the cages and stare out together on the world, separated by bars but joined in a common sympathy.

Yet Kraal grew increasingly irritable as the autumn advanced, and though he would talk to Woil he became ill-tempered with Minch who, he said, spoke a lot but did little.

But this was untrue, for Minch had become quieter and more peaceful as the months had gone by, staring out over the Zoo with a mysterious tranquillity, as if she had found some contentment that eluded the others.

Kraal had long ago warned Creggan that autumn was Slorne's worst time but so far this had not proved so. She still huddled in her small silent way at the top of her cage, watching the trees and sky and never looking at the Zoo, the people, or the other eagles.

But there came an evening warm and still when this changed, and Creggan was shocked by what he saw. It was quite sudden. One moment she was quiet in the corner of the cage and the next she was flying across to the front corner of her cage, frantic with some purpose the bars and wire mesh would never allow her to achieve.

She clashed her talons on the bars, brought her beak down on them as well in a way that must have pained her, and swung sideways towards Creggan. Her eyes were wild and did not seem to see him, her wings were smashing at the bars and branch in her cage, and she was over and up to the top. Faster she did it, and faster, and for Creggan the worst thing was this: agonized and frantic though she was, she never called out or made a sound, yet her beak was open in a silent scream.

'What can we do?' Creggan asked Minch. 'Surely there is something?'

'Later we can calm her, but for now she will continue like this until she grows tired. Each year it is the same and it starts when the black swifts begin to flock and sweep over the Zoo. See, they have come!'

It was true. Beneath and beyond the flocking starlings the evening air was alight with the flight of swifts which wheeled and dived with a speed which dazzled Creggan.

'But why do they upset her?' he asked.

'They are feeding on insects in preparation for the flight south they will soon make. Many of them go to north Africa, where Slorne comes from. And at night it is sometimes possible to hear overhead the migrating flight of other birds going south: flycatcher and greylag, wheatear and nightingale. Their migration must bring to Slorne a terrible longing for the land she was taken from.'

'How do you know this if she never speaks?' Creggan wanted to know.

'It is true that in the eighteen years she has been here I have never heard her speak. But in time, when you live with other eagles, you learn to understand them without words. You learn to feel as they do and begin to see that words may often be in the way of understanding.

'Now, Creggan, you asked me what can be done for Slorne in these autumn weeks of change and frustration. It has always been I who have calmed her, though sometimes the Sweeper has come in the evening and stood for a while at her cage and she has calmed in his good presence. Now I give the task to you.'

With that she said no more but dropped down to her shelter and took up some food, an action that told Creggan he had best get on with it and ask no more questions.

Slorne had already calmed down by the time Creggan and

Minch had finished speaking and the following evening the Sweeper came and she was calm again. Then for a few days she was quiet.

But it did not last long. One evening after the kind of soft autumnal day that is an echo of the summer gone, when the sun sets in the western sky to cast great pinks and reds across its distant clouds, Creggan was peaceful at his stance, dreaming of his own homesite. There was a rush of dark wings across the front of the Cages, and then another, as two swifts cut and raced over the Zoo sky, one moment inches from the Cages, the next chasing airborne insects on the far side of Three Island Pond.

Immediately Slorne grew upset. Whether she had seen those particular swifts Creggan did not know, for she was as usual high at the back of her cage. But perhaps she had seen others at the tree tops, for she clattered her talons violently on the top of her cage, crashed down on to its concrete floor, her wings smashing against the branch that projected across her cage, and then lunged forward at the door of her cage, driven by an impulse that spoke of a terrible longing to be free.

As more swifts swung over the warm evening sky outside she got increasingly agitated and so great was the sound her clashing talons and lunging beak and wild wings made that all the other birds of prey in the Cages grew restless as well. Woil, who was on the other side, stared at her in despair and shared misery before retreating into his shelter.

But Creggan could not escape, for he remembered Minch's command to try and help her, and anyway he could feel the same longings she felt. And he understood her distress.

Home, she wanted to go home. Home, a place he himself had known only briefly. Home . . .

He thought of his own longing for it and of the dream she must have too. He went to the side of her cage, and grasping its bars firmly in his talons he quietly watched her as she raced frantically from corner to far corner of her cage.

What words could he say? He felt as he had that night when he invoked the power of Callanish to intercede and save Minch's life. Then words had come to him from the sky. They began to come to him now.

'There is a land,' he whispered, so quiet that most of what he said was at first drowned by her rushings, 'that lies to the South, beyond a great blue sea. There the skies are bigger than here, and in the evening the sun sets more red, more pink, then ever ours can. And mountains rise above the desert plains and on their sides great forests grow, isolated from man.'

Although the words were his the images were taken from those things Kraal and Minch had told him about that distant place.

'There do your kind fly, Slorne, soaring on the winds that rise up from the hot land, circling over their sites as they seek their prey of mammal and carrion, or chase a black-winged kite from off their food . . .'

Slorne became still and took stance on the branch quite near to Creggan, her head tilting to one side, and her eyes staring out at the sunset sky that rose massively now over the Cages.

'It is a different land where the sun shines bright and in the deserts the rocks are too hot in the day for eagles to land,' he continued. 'There lizards crawl and snakes entwine and smaller birds are colourful. The eagles are the masters of the air, lord over kite and falcon, proud of their rights. To there in spirit can you fly, Slorne, a place where . . .' and his words drifted on as the evening drew into darkness; and she found comfort in them.

After that Creggan often talked to her, sometimes in a barest whisper that only she could hear, and other times more powerfully so that others could share her dream and inner peacefulness. And hearing him Minch was pleased, for she saw that he was learning to understand others and would be ready for the harder lessons she would give him in the coming year.

As autumn progressed the rains came, and storms, and people came less. Everything grew quiet and grey, night came sooner, and the fallen leaves that had bustled brownly on the paths were sodden and began to rot.

The eagles talked less now and fell into their own thoughts as if preparing themselves for the dark months ahead. But sometimes Creggan and Kraal would ask Minch questions and she would speak of things she knew and wisdom she had taught herself or remembered from her distant past at Callanish. But of Callanish itself, which Creggan most wanted to know about, she had refused to speak, saying that the time was not right and she would speak only when it was.

September, October, November . . . and one morning a strange hush came over the Zoo. From somewhere, and none could say quite where, a mist began to drift.

Across the paths it came, in between the cages, around the enclosures, a silent insubstantial sea whose waves left shining moisture where they went.

Creggan found his plumage had fine mist settling on it, while his beak grew shiny wet with it as the trees of Three Island Pond changed to faint grey shadows of their former selves before disappearing into white.

The benches by the Cages were suddenly stark and mysterious as they slowly became set against this drifting whiteness. Sounds grew muffled and footfalls came and went softly and unseen in the mist, from where to where no eagle could tell. Sometimes people or Men changed for a moment into some semblance of shape, but then they moved and the mist drifted and they were gone as if they had never been.

Creggan saw Minch staring intently out into this nothingness, and then drop forward to the front of her cage and look fixedly at the benches, and at the harmless litter bin which Woil had used as a stance during his brief escape. Except it looked harmless no longer. The more Creggan himself stared at it the bigger and stranger it became, looming out of the mist, its grey shrouds entwined round it. The slight tilt it always had now become a great lunge to one side, and as the mist moved against it the bin appeared to be moving the other way.

Creggan grew nervous and glanced over his shoulder and up towards the trees above. They had all disappeared except for one of the bigger branches that bent and pointed a little his way and seemed now to come and go before his very eyes as drifting mist obscured it.

'Callanish! Your Stones have a power as quiet as this . . .'

It was Minch, speaking to some power in the silence. 'Callanish, I can hear you calling out to me . . .' and as she spoke these strange words the looming bench and drifting bin seemed to Creggan to grow larger and taller and darker, and he was afraid.

Then they were aware of something, out there beyond the benches, which they could sense moving silently in the mist, and though he strained to see it he could not quite catch the thing in one place, for it seemed to come and go, larger than the bench and bin, looming nearer but not quite seen, dark and grey and pointing to the sky.

'Now I can speak of Callanish,' Minch continued more slowly, 'where my ancestors flew and where once so long ago I cast my shadow down.'

Instinctively Creggan crept closer to Minch, as did Kraal on the far side of her, trying to catch her whispered words, which seemed to drift as slow and powerful as the mist into which she spoke them.

'He asked me what I could say of you, Callanish, and I waited for your signal knowing that when he was wiser and ready I could tell him.' Creggan held his breath for he knew that though she was speaking of him as if he was not there really it was *she* who had become something else and that some power was using her to speak to him directly.

'Each kind of eagle has its sacred site in whose sanctuary

dark forces weaken and lose their grip. Such is the site of Callanish for the golden eagle and in its circle all may find strength and truth. From that site too come the Callanish eagles whose strength is not in flight, or size, or speed or skill but rather in a spirit whose power has been forged through time.' Her voice became stronger, drifting everywhere like the mist itself.

'Callanish lies in the far north of the Western Isles where sea and land and sky meet as one. It is a low rising hill above the waters of a loch and on it centre powers that only eagles of peace and truth can fully feel.

'There have been eagles there since the far-off days when only the sound of the sea and the call of the curlew broke the peace, before men walked the earth. But it was a place that drew other creatures to its calm, to rest awhile and find their strength again. And these the eagles left unharmed, not seeking them as prey but letting them come and go at will.

'Then men came on boats across the sea and settled on the island, building small homes and taking fish and growing stunted crops. A few sensed the power of Callanish and went there as the creatures did and felt the peace. The eagles debated this coming for years, for in other places men harmed them and drove them away, and they wondered if they should attack the men, even at the sacred site itself.

'But the wisest said No, for men are creatures too and need the powers of Callanish as others do.

'Centuries passed by and the men came and went, and there were long periods when none were there. But then more came, right to the site of Callanish and disturbed it, digging at the soil and making mounds; changing the powers. Then yet more came and brought with them great Stones which one day they started to take to the very centre place of Callanish itself.

'Then did the eagles attack, to stop the men from destroying the site of Callanish. In waves they attacked, driving them back to stop the raising of the Stones which eagles had seen in other places.

'But the men were many and clever and shot at the eagles with arrows, and trapped them in nets and put them to death, one after another. Until at last there was only one Callanish eagle left, a juvenile whom the others had sought to protect and so had prevented from joining in the fighting even though she had wanted to. Alone she saw the last of the adult Callanish eagles fall; alone she watched.

'Then she flew high over the site of Callanish above the men and the fallen bodies of her kind which were scattered over the site. The men gathered to watch her, their arrows and spears ready to kill her, but she flew high, invoking the power of Callanish for advice on how best to attack and take revenge.

'But the powers rebuked her, saying, "This is a site for peace and from it shall peace come. The fight we have witnessed between eagle and man has been fought many times in many places and will be fought again. But here we will make an end of it and leave a sign for all time that it should not be so."

'Then as she circled about she saw a mist come creeping over the sea and across the loch, thick and cold and grey. It encircled the site of Callanish and drifted on to its grassy slopes where the men watched, with their Stones on the shore waiting to be raised.

'Then the mist came nearer until it reached a man and an eagle and before her eyes they turned to stone and were raised up as a single standing stone, to point up into the sky. The mist moved on, and each man and eagle there was turned to stone and raised up. Until at last the whole site was shrouded in thick mist and she could see no more.

'After a while the sun beat down upon the mist and filled it with light and warmth, and a wind blew and the mist thinned and cleared. Then she saw that beneath her on the sacred site of Callanish all of the men and the eagles who had fought had disappeared. In their places were great standing stones, tall and thin and pointing for ever to the sky. They formed a great circle round the very centre of the site, where most eagles had died, and long lines across the moor, pointing to the north, south, east and west, that all who saw them would remember that man and eagle should be as one.

'Then did she fly down to the Stones and among them, grieving for eagles and men alike, who now stood mute around her, pointing as great Stones up to the sky. She asked the powers to make her into a Stone as well but this was not granted. Instead she was told she must find a mate to make a site near by and start a new race of Callanish eagles. And so she did, to watch over the site and guard it from dark forces.

'Then other men came and other eagles, and seeing the Stones they were at peace there and did not harm each other.'

Minch finished speaking, still facing out towards the benches. It seemed to Creggan that she was surrounded by a powerful diffused light until he saw the mist was thinning and the sun beginning to shine. As it did the benches became the benches they had always been, and the litter bin no more than it simply was.

While just behind it, standing still and staring towards Minch's cage, the shape that had seemed to loom so large, as if it was one of the standing stones of which Minch had been speaking, became the shape of a man. And one he knew.

It was the Sweeper.

*

Mr Helmut Wolski stood and stared. So thick had the mist become that he had almost lost his way and hoping to hear the call of one of the animals to orientate himself had heard an eagle's call, and one he knew well. She was calling out into the mist and he listened and did not move. For it seemed to him that the benches and bin he suddenly saw were bigger than normal and that behind them there loomed not the curves and familiar shapes of the black-painted Victorian

Cages, but greater shapes that pointed darkly to the sky as mist enshrouded them in grey and made them seem alive. They seemed like a great group of standing stones upon a misty moor and he wanted to step forward and go to where they were.

Then the sun came through, and light brightened, and the standing dream that Wolski had seen seemed to drift away into memory and he found himself staring into the eyes of the old female golden eagle. And whatever it was she might have said, had she had human words, it spoke of peace, and said they were not enemies. And nodding his head in agreement with that, Mr Wolski took his broom and went off down the path away from the Cages, for it saddened him more and more to see the eagles there.

Yet later, when the mist had gone and a watery sun shone briefly in the sky, he felt a new elation in his kindly heart. He was beginning to feel, to really feel, that the long shadows of his own wartime experience were finally leaving him. Life, as he had once said to the Zoo Curator, *was* wonderful and a man had best enjoy it while he may. And he understood that in that enjoyment would lie his final freedom from a death camp called Sobibor whose memory had remained as the bars to his personal cage decades after its walls and huts and grim enclosures had been overtaken again by a Polish forest. One day, thought Mr Wolski to himself looking around the Zoo, this place will no longer exist, but long before then *I* will have left it, oh yes! And Mr Wolski did something he had never done in the Zoo before: he whistled the tune of a childhood song while he worked.

PART TWO

ESCAPE

9

It was March, and two long hard years had passed. The Zoo lay under a bitter stormy sky, the bars of the cages seeming even more black against it than they were and the leafless trees more bleak. There had been thick snow the previous week, the final throes of winter, and then it had thawed leaving dampness and mud everywhere. Now it was suddenly icy cold again, the wind sending sharp thrusting stabs wherever it could.

The animals huddled in cold misery. Those with warm indoor quarters sought out their warmest nooks, while others, like the eagles, did their best to find refuge in their open shelters looking out from the frozen draughty shadows on to a bitter world.

There were no people about. Even across the Park beyond the main fence of the Zoo, over which the eagles could see if they braved the cold and stared out from the top of their cages, there was not a single person. Only muddy wastes of sodden grass and the occasional patch of grubby snow in some north-facing dark ditch or nook. There were leafless trees, empty park benches and a rising wind that scurried harshly in the frozen emptiness.

Yet here and there in the Park, for those creatures with the inclination to look and take note, the first secret signs of spring were showing through. Hidden among the scrubland by a woody lake were the tiny flowers of yellow winter aconite, and thrusting up through the muddy ground beneath an urban hedge a delicacy of white snowdrops. While quite unmoved by the blasting bitter wind the buff yellow catkins

of an alder tree by a forgotten ditch told that the weather
would be warmer soon.

Two springs, two summers, and now a third winter had
passed by since Woil had made his brief escape into freedom.
Years in which Creggan had matured, his wings bigger now
and darker; years to grow tired of the teachings of old Minch
and bitter that the early hopes of freedom he had had were
gone.

Minch had seemed to change. She had become tougher on
Creggan, saying that he must use what little space there was
in his cage to practise flight – turning, wheeling, lifting
himself again and again and again . . . for she said that the
day might come when he would need those skills. He would
not survive in the open if he had no strength.

'Survive? The open? Flight?' He had shouted bitterly at
her more than once. 'Oh, I shall survive all right! Here, where
you and the others have survived, for decades, where there
is no danger and no hope.'

But Minch ignored these outbursts, willing him quietly on.
For in her heart she trusted the powers of Callanish that had
spoken to her and she believed the day would come when he
would go free. She did not know of the vow he had made
that if it ever did come he would make sure she was the first
to go, even if it meant him staying in the Cages. And despite
all his anger he never spoke of it. It was a pact he had made
within himself, and with those powers, if they existed, known
as Callanish.

The wind rattled at the bars and made the doors of the
Cages shake and squeak. Powder snow swept in chill flurries
along the black path by the Cages, while above the wind
shrilled in the swaying trees, harsh and irregular. Nothing
much to see, even less to do.

Hours passed and the wind worsened to the strongest it
had been for days. The trees over Three Island Pond bent to
the left with its force, and Creggan saw from the shadows
that such ducks as were visible were taking shelter on the lee

of the islands, bunching together for warmth and sinking their necks and heads as far as they could into their breast feathers. The wind made little waves on the pond, which lapped coldly on the shore. Somewhere something fell with a bang and a man cursed, the harsh sounds swallowed by the wind.

*

Mr Wolski had finished for the day. He had spent most of it indoors in the research laboratories where three offices were being cleared out, stripped and redecorated. As the heating was off it had been cold, but he had comforted himself with the thought that it was not as cold as it was outside where many of the animals were.

The offices faced out on to the wolf enclosure and as he looked at the pack huddled by the iron fence in the snow he thought how right they looked for once. Their grey sandy fur was ruffed out for warmth and occasionally he saw the snarl of their teeth as they turned for a moment on each other in play. Their enclosure ran right along the side of the Park, which he could see beyond, stretching wanly into the distance with London's high-rise buildings far behind. With a wry smile he thought to himself that all it needed was a few thousand square miles of northern forest such as might be found in Norway or Canada and they would look *completely* right.

He said so to the Zoo Curator, who was in that building in the afternoon, adding, 'Naturally, there would have to be no bars there, Curator! None at all!'

The Curator had laughed and told him, 'Mr Wolski, you really are a bit of a revolutionary you know. I sometimes think that you would be happier working somewhere else!'

The Curator did not see the look in Mr Wolski's eyes as he glanced back to the window and stared again at the wolves outside, who had turned to face the icy wind with narrowed yellow eyes. A look of imprisonment and confinement which spoke of a need to escape every bit as strong as that felt by the eagles.

'Ah, but who would want an old man like me who is not even English! Even after all these years my English is not so good and I like still honeycake better than your heavy Christmas pudding!'

The Curator laughed again and then looked serious. 'I was only joking, you know, Mr Wolski. You are very valuable to us here. You know more about the ways of animals and how to handle them than most of the youngsters we get working here now.' And Mr Wolski had nodded and been pleased to hear that said.

Now the day was over and it was getting dark outside and the Zoo would soon be closed. As he often did, Mr Wolski headed for the staff exit the long way round, by way of the Cages. The wind was strong and darkness coming nearer by the second. Ice was forming on Three Island Pond. Everything seemed to rattle and shake, bend and toss as the wind clutched at the neck of his coat and the buttons of his shirt, sending chilly fingers down his chest and worrying at his wrists and hands with its cold.

The golden eagles were sheltering, the buzzard was tucked away out of sight, and the fish eagle was pecking in a half-hearted way at his food on the floor of the shelter.

Only one of the eagles was out, and that was the tawny eagle, which was strange, since in this weather she was usually the first to take shelter. What was stranger still was that she seemed stressed and worried, and kept raising her wings into the wind and bending forward at it and then letting it lift her off her stand to the top of her cage where she stuck out her talons, hovered for a moment and then flopped inelegantly down again to the bare branch.

At first she did not notice him standing there near her cage in the darkening gloom but when she did she did something he had never seen her do in all the years he had watched her.

She lunged forward at him, striking her talons on the bars where his face might have been and crashing her beak thunderously down. He spoke in a calm voice to her for he thought that the wind was upsetting her, but she took no notice and came at him again, and again. It was as if she did not want him there. Wolski shuddered at the grim scene, made worse by this normally peaceful African tawny eagle being angry and stressed over nothing he could see. He came forward speaking softly but this only made it worse, for she came at him again, this time so viciously that, thinking she might hurt herself, he backed away across the path towards the benches.

Then the old female golden eagle came out into the gloom to see what the fuss was.

For a few moments she stared at the tawny eagle and then at Mr Wolski, and he looked at her. And then, it seemed to him, some power possessed her for she too hissed and struck out at him. As if she too did not want him there, not then, not at that moment.

He backed away, and still they struck and lunged in his direction; he backed away even more until he could barely see them in the gloom.

Only the line of grim cages among whose bars whined the winter wind, and above them the great plane trees that bent across the sky, their leafless branches bending in the wind like twisted hands that came down towards him from the angry sky.

Shaking his head sadly at the stark scene he turned to head for the Zoo's exit. But as he did the wind caught at him even more mightily than before; there was the sense of commotion and movement in the air and out of the darkness behind him came a terrible crack, a heave and a bang and whoosh such as he had never heard in his life.

He turned and looked back and saw that where the eagles were, especially the central cages where the golden eagles lived, there was chaos. A branch of the great plane tree had

come down in the wind and as he ran back towards the Cages
he saw that it had fallen right across the path where moments
before he had been standing. Where he might have been
standing still had not the eagles lunged at him, as if moments
before it fell they had sensed that some danger was there and
had sought to protect him.

*

The first Creggan knew of the falling branch was the crack it
made, loud and violent and cutting right into his chilly
reverie as he huddled in his shelter preparing for the night.
The Sweeper had come by, Slorne was upset about something,
then Minch . . . and he beginning to wake to the sense that
something was going to happen, something . . . and then the
CRACK! And even as its sound struck the cage about him,
there was a crash and a judder and the sky was falling in
upon him from the darkening night.

He mantled his wings automatically and thrust his head
forward aggressively, obeying a deep instinct to protect
himself from danger.

'Creggan! Creggan!'

It was Minch's voice calling out anxiously to him.

Creggan came out of his concrete shelter into his cage, the
branch thrust right over it and on to the path in front, and
smaller branches from it filling half his cage with confusion.

Minch was staring at him, the bars between them buckled
and bent.

Creggan began to say, 'What's happened . . .?' but he
stopped in awe as he looked about him and up to where the
branch had fallen and saw something strange and suddenly
frightening. It cast in him a fear so deep that he could say
nothing, only stare.

For above him was an open sky. No bars, no wire mesh,
nothing. A vast impenetrable openness which froze him to
the spot where he was as if he was caught in ice.

'Creggan, Creggan!' But their voices were distant, coming

from another world, Minch and Woil, and Kraal all were calling; but he could not respond. Only stare up at the gaping hole in his cage and feel the terror of the sky beyond and look at where the broken end of the great branch that had fallen spiked out into the wild sky above as its broken part lay about him, its smaller branches and torn bark fretting on the cold wind.

'Creggan, Creggan . . .' and the voices called out still. And the running feet of Men, and the opening of iron doors, and keys and Men's voices.

In a daze of fear and dread at the vast sky that hung above him Creggan looked around at the Cages. The Men were outside his cage trying to open it but failing because the branch had buckled it. Minch and Kraal were calling. Slorne was huddled silently in the top corner of her cage looking at the sky.

Then he heard Minch's voice, angry and authoritative.

'Creggan, can you hear me, Creggan?'

He nodded vaguely.

'Now has your moment come. NOW, Creggan, is the time we have been waiting for. Do not be afraid. Remember how Woil was recaptured because of his fear. Fly up now before it is too late. For the Men are there at your door . . .'

'. . . and another on the roof of the Cages with a net . . .' It was Woil's voice, desperate to see the same fear that had stopped him finding freedom now overtaking Creggan.

Unwillingly, and forced up only by the power in Minch's voice, Creggan flew up to his normal place, nearer to the terrible open sky. The wind blew and the broken bars and bent mesh swayed about him. The plane tree above seemed dark and sinister. So near, so near was the freedom of the sky . . . but across such a terrible void of fear.

'Up, Creggan, UP! They're opening the door now, they're coming over the roof with a net. NOW, Creggan.'

Up he went again, a little nearer, taking stance on one of

the smaller branches of the bough that had fallen, the fresh bark feeling soft and strange to his grip. New, and threatening.

He peered upwards to that terrible sky across which great clouds seemed to race, dark and sinister; rushing and too vast for him, their undersides turned livid by distant city lights.

'Go ON, Creggan. Go ON!' His friends were calling to him, urging him on, and he was thinking that if this was what he had wanted all these years he was afraid of it. It was too big for him.

'I can't,' he whispered. 'I can't raise my wings to that sky. It is too vast, I do not have the courage, I do not know how.' As he said these words he remembered again the vow he had made to the powers of Callanish which was that he would let Minch go before him. He stared wildly up at her cage roof but though it was buckled by the fall of the tree branch it was still intact and she could not escape. He could not leave her here even had he the courage to go up into that vast nothingness above . . .

As he thought of this he grasped on to it with relief for it seemed to give him a reason to do nothing, though in his heart he knew it was fear, not duty, that prevented him from flying.

'Go on, Creggan, NOW Creggan; they will have the net over the hole in your cage. GO ON GO ON GO ON . . .' their voices seemed as harsh and frightening as the sky and as chilly cold as the wind and whatever they said he couldn't, he knew he couldn't. He could see the Men coming, the Men nearly through the bent door, the Man crawling across the roof, and Men coaxing, their voices soft and alluring; safe and secure. He couldn't rise into that great openness which was only inches above his head where the wind blew free . . . and especially not with that vow he had made holding him back.

In that moment Creggan came near to spiritual death. His head dropped, his wings sagged, and he gave up any attempt

to fly out, not just then but ever. He felt the full force of his
own weakness, and he had strength no more to fight, not
without support, not without help . . .

And then help came. From out of the terrible confusion
came a different voice, a gentle voice, a voice that understood.

It was the barest whisper and yet he could hear it clearer
than all the others for it seemed to make everything else fade
away. It came from his left, near by, and he looked there and
found that Slorne was just the other side of the bars from him
and she was looking at him. From some depth of courage and
purpose she who had been silent so long was finding the will
to speak at last.

'There is a land,' she was whispering, each word seeming
difficult for her, each word needing courage, 'there is a place
to the north of here, far to the north, where red deer range
and your kind fly free. It is better than this place, Creggan,
and you can fly to it. It is your land, Creggan, it is yours . . .'
and she spoke to him gently as so often in the past he had
spoken to her. And just as she had found peace in his words,
so did he in hers now. Peace and time. For it was as if the
confusion was gone and it was they – the Men, the wind, the
voices of the others, that were slowing, and he who had all
the time he needed.

'If the vow you made that night for Minch's safe return is
holding you back do not let it, for there are many ways such
a vow may be fulfilled,' she said. 'Minch's freedom will fly in
your wings. Trust the powers that have brought you this
chance, trust your strength, trust in your love of Minch and
your memory of all of us. These things will guide you.

'Now raise your wings, my dearest friend,' whispered
Slorne, 'and be proud, for in them you carry the hopes of all
of us. In them you carry the anger of Kraal and the cunning
of Woil, and the wisdom of Minch. All who have taught you
in their different ways. From me you take the love of home
to put it in whatever place you make your own. Fly now,
Creggan, and fly like the eagle we all might be. But if ever

there is a chance, send us a sign that you are free and have made a place. Only send us a sign . . .'

And as the Men broke through into his cage and reached up to grab him, and as another started to throw a net over the hole in the cage above, so Creggan flexed his wings, thrust forward and up and surged out above his friends and the Cages into the wild forbidding sky, and freedom.

10

As Creggan soared upwards he found himself lost in a swirling black wind in which were scattered moving lights, swaying trees and strange sounds he had never heard before. It took him several long moments to work out where ground was, where sky was, and where *he* was.

Even as he did get his bearings a great tree swirled towards him out of the night and a rook he never saw rose up in alarm, cawing darkly away into the storm. The tree's branches clutched at him out of the darkness and he floundered up in an attempt to get clear of them. Then up and on again with the wild wind catching at his wings and he trying to control it, to hover and reorientate.

To his relief he found he was above the trees and looking down into a murkiness that was beginning to map itself below him into defined and recognizable shapes. To his right wing the Zoo stretched away in the distance; Three Island Pond he recognized as a paler shape than the rest with lights on the paths around to mark it out; the Cages were in front of it with several Men around them. Across the centre of the Cages was the fallen branch.

To his left wing he could see the great blackness of the Park, lit only occasionally by murky yellow lights. While ahead were the threatening lights of houses and cars going round the perimeter of the Park.

The wind caught at him, blew at him, a gusty enemy he found he could hardly overcome. A tilt to the left and it had taken his wing and was driving him back down to the ground;

correction to the right and it was at him that way, turning him round and out of control.

Creggan was more afraid than he could ever remember, and did not know where to go and what to do.

To think . . . he had to think. He could not go near the lights for the Men would see him; so he would seek the most darkness – away from the Zoo and over towards the blackness of the Park centre. He swung that way, no more than a hundred feet above a path, watching forward for trees and obstructions. He would find somewhere high to take stance and think. It had to be high enough to be out of reach of the Men, for they could not fly. He remembered Woil staying by the bench and the litter bin where the Men could reach him. He would not make that mistake.

He turned instinctively against the wind, or nearly, for that way was easiest to control, and fortunately it took him towards the greatest darkness. There was a rushing sound ahead like great waves of wind.

'Trees,' he muttered to himself. 'Trees! High and safe! The place to go.' In seconds he found himself hovering over a group of them which swayed this way and that beneath him in the dark, not nice and firm like the dead branch set in his cage.

The wind whipped at him, making it hard to hover and harder still to drop his talons on the moving branches on which he was trying to land. He tried, and felt himself falling into the tree, confused, unable to find a stance that did not give way into clutching twigs and flailing branches. He had to beat his wings painfully against obstructions to fight his way out again.

Creggan moved on through the night wind. The rough ground and trees beneath changed into the flatness of water. A lake. A wooden building near it. Thankfully he landed on it for a moment, moving his body back and forth to keep balance with the stress of the wind and peering about him.

'Mustn't panic, mustn't rush. No Man here. Safe for the

moment.' To his alarm he found that the brief flight had utterly exhausted him.

A shadow moved by a light ahead on a path. Man. But not one of *them*. He could tell by the clothes. But taking no risks he rose again into the night. Another group of trees on the far side of the lake and lights on the edge of the Park again. So much ground covered so fast. Below, a tree, broken, not so many branches. Easier, easier . . . and Creggan, with his talons tentatively stretched out below him, landed on one of its branches.

The tree swayed beneath him, every branch, every twig seeming to move differently, and all whimpering, whining and stressing in the wind. Sometimes a sharp crack and something falling into darkness. Confusing. Breathing heavily from tiredness Creggan muttered instructions to himself. He needed to rest and think, and then to plan.

There were no lights near by or below him but he could see the lake stretching into the night off to the left, its surface catching the lights of the buildings and city sky over by the edge of the Park. He decided to stay where he was.

It was a long night, and one Creggan never forgot. He could not seem to sleep or rest for fear that some danger would come from which he would have to flee. But nothing came and a little before dawn the wind eased and he managed to close his eyes in the shelter of the old oak tree in which he had taken stance.

When he woke it was suddenly, and to a sight of beauty he had never dreamed he might see. It was dawn and the storm was quite over. A weak sun was rising off to the east over the distant buildings and its pale light was filtering through the branches of the trees about him. As the seconds stretched into minutes so the advance of the soft light across the park unfolded beneath him. Before his eyes dull muddy grass turned into soft reflective banks which caught the sun a thousand ways. Bleak black branches suddenly shone with the colours of dark red buds, of shining bark, of pale dry trunks that caught the sun and held it in their sinuous heights.

And the sound! Not the clankings and gratings of the Zoo which lay off in the distance to his right, now obscured by the trees over which he had flown in the night, but the call of a thousand birds whose busyness and life shook his fears off him for a time and replaced them with a sense of wonder.

A sudden urgent flight of Canada geese overhead directed his gaze to the lake that stretched westward towards the houses. He followed their swift line as together they swung low over the water and landed, the splash of their coming rippling softly back to him on the still air.

There was a vast murmur of duck-talk on the lake as he made out group after group, some in the water and some on the banks, busy and preoccupied with feeding. Five mallard shot past the tree in which he was hidden, their muttered quacks in mid-air soft as the sun that crept the way they were going and began to fill the lake with light.

A Man. Two Men. He recognized them by the bright overalls they wore. Across the Park near some trees were two more, from the direction of the Zoo. Four Men. He sensed danger and threat. He tried not to panic. If he moved they would see him; if he stayed still they would find him. Better to stay still . . . it would take them time to catch him here . . .

But it did not work. Out of a group of trees near by a rook flew, winging its way leisurely across the Park towards him. Nearer. Creggan stared at it. It came nearer still until it saw him. If it had been possible for a bird to stop still with surprise in the air, and stay exactly where it was, that rook would have done it then. An eagle! An *eagle*!

It called out in alarm, turned, raced back to where it had come from and then disappeared. Then by some sinister magic other rooks appeared from nowhere; two, three; six . . . coming towards him.

Creggan took flight into the air but they made straight for him. Their caws were threatening. He felt the air in his wings as he stretched out over the sky; he felt his strength. Then the rooks were on him, mobbing him, diving at him blackly from all directions. He twisted and turned but still they came at him. He struck out at them and soared upwards and they fell away for a time. Then back they came, again and again.

Other birds scattered away below; blackbirds and thrushes, sparrows and robins. The sky was commanded by an eagle and rooks. After a time Creggan felt no more fear, merely weariness. He could outmanoeuvre them if he wished but he could not get rid of them and he was only groping round in circles about the tree he had made his own.

He landed again and they lurked near by, staring, watching, waiting blackly. He saw the Men had come nearer. They had seen him. He decided to stay where he was to see what would happen. With one sweep of his wings he could rise up into the sky and out of their grasp.

*

Mr Wolski was among the group of keepers who first saw the escaped golden eagle. The poor bewildered creature was being mobbed by rooks. The keepers had nets and baited meat which they hoped he would take . . .

Mr Wolski did not want the eagle caught but he knew its chances of escape were very low. It would be confused and afraid, and would not know how to find food. It would take the easy way and go for the baited food laid out for it . . .

Mr Wolski followed the keepers with a heavy heart. They reached the tree where the eagle had taken stance and looked up. So many voices shouting 'Climb up!' 'Lay out food!' 'Wait for a time!' 'Don't alarm him!' 'Stand still!' Mr Wolski could not help remembering a time when he had been a fugitive outside the fences of Sobibor in the scrubland of the Parczew Forest. He had heard shouts like these then, and the bark of dogs, and the cries and screams as Jewish friends near by were found and summarily shot. He had lain quite still then and it had worked. He had not been found.

Now Mr Wolski smiled. The keepers were more confused than the eagle was. If the eagle did nothing and waited they would not get him. He just needs time, thought Mr Wolski.

At nine thirty the first journalist arrived. He had a photographer with him and was from a daily newspaper. At ten the second came. At eleven the first TV film crew turned up. By twelve there were eighteen journalists, eight photographers, two film crews, and ten frustrated and annoyed keepers under Creggan's tree.

*

It did not take Creggan long to work out that the Men couldn't reach him. They stared at him, he stared at them. Sometimes he looked round the Park to see if he might move somewhere else but he did not like to start a flight with so many Men staring at him all at once. The people had black things which clicked, like they did in the Zoo sometimes.

But finally deciding it was time to move off, and doing his best to ignore the rooks, which began to mob him again the moment he took flight, he flew three hundred yards to another oak which he had been looking at with some care. This time he had no trouble landing. He watched curiously as the Men and the People followed him across the field and over the fence which the tree was beyond. They grouped under his tree again. After a while one of the Men began climbing the tree.

Creggan did not like this and flew back to the first tree. The Men and the People followed him back across the Park. There seemed to be more of them collecting by the minute. They were muttering and making sounds as the Men did when they were angry.

He saw them lay out food on the grass beneath both trees. Having eaten well the day before he was not hungry and anyway did not trust the Men. He would not touch their food.

Creggan decided to fly to the far side of the lake. He was getting used to the rooks and had more confidence in the air and in landing among the branches of a tree. For a time the Men left him alone, but eventually they caught up with him. The day passed. He chose a stance high up in a plane tree where he knew that if they tried climbing he would see them long before they reached him. Night fell.

There were lights below, and lights shining up at him. He did not like it. He flew away silently over the trees. The Men were left behind.

*

Next day Mr Wolski found that several of the morning newspapers had pictures of the golden eagle on their front page.

'FLIGHT TO FREEDOM' read the headline of one over a picture of the unusual sight of a golden eagle flying over Regent's Park. Mr Wolski had enjoyed the television news the night before which showed the Curator being interviewed and pictures of the eagle flying from tree to tree and a lot of journalists getting their shoes and trousers muddy.

But he was concerned as well. He knew that the young eagle would get hungry and would need food. The eagle had never hunted and surely would not know how. It seemed inevitable that he would take the bait that had been laid out in the Park for him. Then he would be lured and caught . . .

Mr Wolski sighed. He knew himself that it is one thing to get out of prison, another really to escape it.

*

By the fourth day Creggan was very hungry indeed. He was also getting more tired. He knew he could survive without ill effect for a week or more without food but he sensed he was weakening. He could see the food the Men had laid out in different places across the Park and he was tempted by it; and the thought of its taste began to obsess him. Perhaps it was not dangerous. Perhaps they were being kind and he could have a bit, just a little . . .

On the morning of the fourth day, with Men and People still in pursuit wherever he went, Creggan headed for a place where the food was where no Men were near. He swooped down on to the grass and took stance by it. He stabbed at it with his talons and beak. He took it up and flew to a stance on one of the wooden buildings round the Park. He wanted the food. Just a taste. Yet he hesitated: would an eagle like Kraal have even risked it? Anyway, it felt weak and wrong to be free and still take the Men's food. He let it slither down the roof to the building's guttering. He would have to find his own food.

All day he searched, trying to see a prey he could take. His attention settled on the ducks on the lake but whenever he got near they fled in panic to the shore and sheltered under bushes and trees where he could not reach them. He realized that if he was to be successful he would have to take them at speed.

Hunger. It gnawed at him as he wanted to gnaw at food. It overtook him. It made him angry and irritable. The rooks, the Men, the staring People, all made him angry. And beneath his hunger was fear. For he knew he must act fast now, and more than that, that the time was coming when if he was really to escape he must leave the protection of the Park and venture north over the great city whose houses frightened him.

Evening, and warmer air now with lighter winds. Again he dived over the lake, and again the rooks chased him and the ducks fled. He must think, and plan. He must know what he was doing.

All night he thought, all night he planned. Early in the morning, in the grey cold light that precedes the rising sun, he positioned himself in trees to the east of the lake but out of sight of it. He waited. Thin sun came. He took off, wheeled round with the sun behind him and kept low over the trees. The sound of the waking ducks was below him in the scrub and trees. Some were already out on the lake, quiet and dabbling. He fixed his stare on a shelduck whose white and brown plumage he could easily see. He gathered speed with a slight adjustment of his wings, soaring inches over the tree tops, the air rushing audibly in his feathers. The last of the trees fell away behind him, the lake rushed forwards below, the shelduck dabbled on unaware.

Creggan felt power in his wings, and control. He swung his talons powerfully forward in the way Minch and Kraal had often described, he pulled back his wings to drop faster through the air, he pushed down towards the shelduck and with a great splash and spray of water took the bird powerfully in his talons. It was dead from shock before Creggan had started a single beat of his wings to rise again over the lake. In that moment he felt alive and powerful. The rooks came out to mob him but they were nothing, nor were the Men.

He took stance in a high tree to pluck and eat his prey. The feathers floated away from him on the light breeze, catching at the grey budding branches of the tree beneath him, drifting down to where the few Men and People who were there looked helplessly up. He ate slowly and surely. He had time, and he had strength. And in taking prey for the first time he had found courage.

He dropped the remnant carcase of his prey and pushed up into the fresh morning sky. He soared higher, and higher, and the Men and the People, and finally the rooks, fell away far beneath him. The Park was a small thing below, and the Zoo an even smaller part of it. He turned and looked north. The city stretched for miles. But here and there were outcrops of green which would be places to rest and hunt. While through the spring haze yet further north, he could see hills of green where the city stopped.

He circled once more on the mild wind and finally, without looking back, he set course to the north, to try to find the distant beloved place called Cape Wrath where once, so long ago, he had been born.

*

As he entered the Zoo Mr Wolski whistled with pleasure, though he knew he shouldn't. It was unfortunate when a zoo lost an eagle, so why did he feel so pleased about it? Well, he knew perfectly well why, so he whistled some more just for fun. His only regret was that it was not his old friend the female golden eagle who had escaped.

Mr Wolski knew what he was going to do at lunchtime that fine spring day. He was going to eat his sandwiches and read again his copy of the *Daily Mirror*, which had across its centre spread a picture of an eagle. The headline, in very large letters indeed, read 'FIRST KILL!' and it showed the golden eagle taking a duck on the lake in Regent's Park. And the words that went with it said that 'after enjoying a leisurely breakfast the eagle soared high over the park and set course north, towards Scotland, where golden eagles come from. And good luck to him!'

A thought with which Mr Wolski silently agreed.

11

As Creggan turned north away from the Park all he could see for miles ahead was the stretching city. Men's houses and roads, with centipedes of cars threading along them, and tiny milling people like the ants that came in the summer in the far corner of his cage. There were a few areas of welcome grassland like the one that rose ahead of him almost as soon as he left the Park behind. But he did not stop and it faded back into houses again below him as he pressed on.

There was a perpetual hum from the ground below, and occasional harsher metallic bangs and scrapes, and judders of thick silvery snakes that sped along faster than cars and disappeared into black holes in the ground. Planes roared above, and had he not got used to their sound from his years in the Zoo he might have been afraid of them. Once a smaller one buzzed by like a transparent bumble bee, below him but still above the tallest buildings. He was wary of it, thinking it might be living, but he saw it was just another machine.

The roads made winding patterns below, the houses arrayed along them, and if he soared higher the noises of Men faded. He could see to his left wing in the distance more open country, but his sense of north was strong and his instinct to follow it stronger.

As he flew he made his plans. He would stop before he got tired. He would seek out a place away from Men. He would travel slowly. He would learn.

Occasionally two or three rooks would straggle up to mob him from some tree or tiny patch of parkland they were trying to protect but he was going strongly and the wind was giving him support and direction.

Once he saw a great swirling mass of gulls and rooks over a messy area of what seemed upturned soil and rubbish. He sensed food, but there were Men there and great machines. He pressed on.

The houses thinned below him, there were more trees and areas of park and an area of bare soil with hundreds of thin parallel lines on it. Then a group of lakes too patterned to be natural. He was beginning to have a sense of Man things and natural things. Man things were regular and patterned, and cut across the contours of the country and the flow of things. A road goes straight, rivers meander; houses are in straight lines, trees irregular.

But patterned though the country was – cut into straight-sided fields, dissected by ditches which ignored natural lines, crossed by lines of wired poles – it was getting greener by the mile. To his left wing he made out a line of higher hills and headed for it. Rooks streamed up towards him from a small area of woodland. He veered higher over another kind of wood whose trees he did not know but which had lighter bark and were higher. No rooks there.

He took stance near the top of a tree and rested. But the weather had darkened a little and so he quickly pressed on, anxious to get the city as far behind him as possible. The hills he had come to had a clear line running south-west to north-east and he turned that way. It was not direct north but what interested him were the air currents the hills created. To his right wing the hills sloped gently down and were of little interest but on his left they formed a steep escarpment up whose side came a soaring wind. Its line was quite clear and he needed only to veer a little into it and he felt enormous uplift under his wings and a lightness and power unlike anything he had felt in the Park.

He progressed north-east, using the uplift warily at first but then with increasing confidence, soaring round and round in its rising power and powering forward for miles, until he saw the hills begin to falter ahead and the ground to flatten unpromisingly. Creggan was beginning to read the windscape around him and to plan a route by it.

He might have pressed on but the sight of a group of hassling crows on a chalk slope below attracted him. They were at carrion and he was hungry.

Creggan stooped down and hovered for a moment over the carrion. It was a dead sheep. The crows scuttled off, their cawings loose on the scarp breeze. He settled near the sheep, side-stepped to it, and started to feed. Sometimes he left the food, leaned into the wind and took off for a while, to circle and check that no Men were about. But there were none, and only an occasional crow worried him. While lower on the slope a group of sheep, seeming to sense his presence, bunched together and moved off.

Creggan might have stayed longer but that he became aware of a man silhouetted on the skyline. He took off, flying low and keeping out of sight, tilting quickly up above a treeline to check what he had seen and then dipping out of sight again. He was becoming cunning and learning how to survive. He began to look for a safe stance for the night . . .

*

Mr Helmut Wolski had felt a different man since the golden eagle's escape, and now did some things differently. One of them was that he opened his morning newspaper with an enthusiasm he had not felt for years. For like millions of other readers he was following the slow northward progress of the escaped eagle as it was reported day by day in most of the popular newspapers.

The eagle had been sighted at various points all over the British Isles by enthusiastic birdwatchers, most of them amateurs. So varied were the locations – from Cornwall to Wales, from Somerset to Kent, that most could be discounted. There was even a report from three sea anglers off Folkestone who saw the eagle heading south-west over the Channel towards France.

But the more reliable sightings, by experienced observers, showed that the eagle was going northwards. Mr Wolski had already read the accounts of him being seen over the Chiltern Hills north-west of London soon after leaving the Regent's Park area, and later a certain sighting by a member of the Royal Society for the Protection of Birds in East Anglia who saw him feeding off sheep carrion on chalk downland.

So excited had Mr Wolski become – though he kept quiet about it at the Zoo – that he had taken down his atlas of the British Isles so he could mark off the various places the eagle was seen.

A pattern was beginning to emerge. After three days' disappearance following the sheep-eating incident, the eagle was seen again for certain on a telegraph pole outside the village of Lutterworth near Leicester by a passing motorist, Mrs Gillian Cook. Her description was so detailed and precise that experts agreed that she had seen the eagle.

The story had been taken up in yesterday's paper by another lady, old-age pensioner Miss Judith Kennedy, a retired teacher who told a local reporter that 'I know an eagle when I see one because I lived in Cyprus for twenty years and there are many eagles there. This one was definitely a golden eagle and in good condition. It was feeding near a local rubbish dump and I did not attempt to approach it since there's a barbed wire fence round the dump and I am seventy-three and no longer climb fences. Anyway, it should be left in peace.'

Eagle-spotting was becoming a national pastime and experts on birds of prey suddenly found themselves being quoted in every paper or interviewed on radio and television. As Mr Wolski ate his usual morning toast and marmalade he was listening to a spokesman from the RSPB saying, 'We think it possible that the eagle will try to find high ground. He will be less disturbed there and might find it easier to get prey. Fortunately the weather is mild and spring has set in which means that there will be prey about – young mammals and so on. If a member of the public sees him then they should on no account approach him or make a disturbance. The bird's survival so far is remarkable, but his chances improve each day as he learns more about his new environment . . .'

Mr Wolski was interested in this because he himself had seen the RSPB man at the Zoo yesterday and had heard unofficially that their real worry was that someone might try to trap or shoot the bird. This had already happened to many birds of prey and there were still farmers around who believed that eagles took live lambs, though the evidence was very slight.

Mr Wolski stared at his map. Only forty miles ahead of the previous sighting lay the beginnings of the great Pennine range, the backbone of England. If the eagle could only reach there in safety he would have a chance of following almost continuous high ground to Scotland . . .

*

Although Creggan had progressed northwards well, he had slowed during the last day or two as he grew tired easily and rested by feeding off rubbish dumps he had seen where gulls and crows fed. They did not like his presence but he found little difficulty in scaring them off, or evading them if they tried to mob him, and the food in these places was plentiful.

But he was troubled by the proximity of houses and ahead by the evidence of industry and a pall of haze and smoke in the air. The area seemed almost worse than the city he had left, and the metallic noise and traffic hum that came up from it was more formidable.

But the weather was mild and encouraging, and he felt the pull of the North, and the need for high ground. At the same time he was anxious to see his first raven, for he remembered Woil saying that the ravens started 'where the mountains start, and their range spreads ever northwards to the very heart of eagle and buzzard country'.

So very early one morning when the wind was a moderate westerly and made northward progress easy, Creggan set off over the great industrial cities to find the high ground beyond them that he sensed would be there.

He flew slowly and high, watching the land unfold beneath him as buildings and roads gave way to brief outcrops of country followed by more towns. The ground got steadily hillier, and here and there rock outcrops stood out which, had they not been so near to towns, he would have been tempted to investigate. He felt strong and wanted more and more to reach somewhere that had less evidence of the patterning of Man.

He quickened his flight as he saw ahead in the far distance, perhaps twenty miles on, the blue rising of real hills – ground higher than any he had seen so far. The nearer he got the more the hills below became steeper and wilder, the paths on them fewer, and only rough stone walls patterned them into occasional huge fields. Sheep grazed there and sometimes he would see lambs playing far below. Occasionally too he saw crows flocking and feeding at a particular part of a sheep pasture – sometimes at a dead sheep but more often at the placenta left behind where a lamb had been born.

Again, he might have been tempted to land and feed, but he felt an urging to fly on, to travel far, as if today of all days he would begin to feel freedom at last.

He felt his strength powerfully, and a joy in flight far more real and powerful than the dreams and hopes had made of it in his cage at the Zoo.

The hills below were rising into moorland, vast and brown, on which the sheep roamed more sparsely. There were occasional stark outcrops of rock and dark pools like tiny versions of the lochans he dimly remembered from his homesite. But still in the sky, on either side of the spine of upland, he could see the pall of urban haze that marked Man's towns and cities. He pressed on and on, resting only briefly on a rock outcrop before continuing.

The air was cooler and there were pockets of snow in some of the enshadowed river gullies below him. The vegetation had a dank and wintry look to it still, quite different from the lowlands. There was little life apart from sheep. He saw the occasional pheasant and partridge winging rapidly away beneath him, or skulking in the brown grass and bracken. Here and there were young rabbits on the lower south-facing slopes.

On, on he went. Tiring now but wanting a sign that he had really reached wild ground. A Man-track below petered out, ahead the vegetation broke into bare rock; a loud harsh call on the wind to his right. Black-purple wings in the sky. Black beaks. Wings bigger and blacker and more formidable than any he had yet seen. Harsh calls. A pair of ravens!

With a joy to his flight that evidently surprised and alarmed them he turned and stooped towards them at speed, not to attack them so much as show them that he was a golden eagle and could fly where he pleased. One turned on its back and presented its claws, the other veered off, and Creggan flew between them, his great wings sweeping past them, his speed leaving them gasping, his power leaving them a memory they would never forget. For he was an eagle in flight to the North where his own kind were and no raven nor man would stop him now.

12

Creggan's northward flight slowed soon after he was challenged by the ravens. The moors got higher, the weather worsened, and temperatures fell. At the same time food was becoming harder to find as the mammals and birds he might have caught were kept off the moors or in hibernation by the still unthawed snow which lay bleakly below him.

So he turned eastwards to lower dales and valleys that ran off the uplands to prey on easy marks he found there, like young rabbits and the occasional sheep's carcase. There were a few Men dwellings standing out starkly in the snow but otherwise little sign of people.

His ability to make use of winds and air currents improved each day, and he became increasingly skilled at spotting movement and danger. Any sign of Men and he was off out of sight using the dead ground between rises to stay hidden, and he was careful to rise when he could over ridges where rocks or trees broke the skyline and so camouflaged his presence.

He slowed his flight north to let the milder weather in the south catch up with him. There was time enough for travel, and now he wanted to watch in wonder the slow unfolding of spring beneath him. The thinning and slushing of snow into water; the sudden appearance of frail catkins on the willow and alder that grew in wet gullies and along lower streams; soft blue skies.

He enjoyed the gradual arrival of other birds, travelling northward and up to higher grounds as they too followed the spring; the buoyant thrushes, sudden parties of blue tits in the lower valleys, and the drumming of woodpeckers from out of still leafless woods. While on higher ground the ravens, the rooks and the crows scattered about and black coots scurried at water edges, busy and aggressive.

Creggan had felt the coming of spring before, a coming that overtook his spirit and made it busy and turbulent, but he had never witnessed it so well. Every flight forward was an adventure, every stance he took a place from which to see new things.

Soon after his first brush with ravens he had seen buzzards like Woil in the distance. He did not feel so hostile to them as he did to the ravens, and merely ignored them, overflying them if they came too close but not behaving more aggressively than that. No point in an argument for argument's sake.

What he most looked forward to seeing were others of his kind with whom he could fly and from whom he would learn things. But he knew he would not see them here – they were much further north and anyway he would know he was near them when the crows gave way to a different more sinister corvid – the hooded crows, the vicious crows whose kind had once nearly succeeded in killing Minch when she was trapped near Callanish.

*

It was at the beginning of May, some weeks after he first left, that the Zoo finally gave up hope of recapturing the escaped golden eagle. It had not been sighted for nearly a month – apart from a brief report by a shepherd in Northumberland which sounded like a possibility but was vague – and the Zoo conceded that if he was still alive he could certainly survive like any other golden eagle in the wild. Repairs to the Cages affected by the falling branch were completed and the Zoo's formal admission of defeat came when they moved a Chilean eagle into the golden eagle's old cage.

By this time the newspapers had lost interest, and the route that Mr Wolski had carefully traced each day on his atlas on the basis of news reports ended near Galashiels in the Southern Uplands of Scotland, where a British Trust for

Ornithology report gave a good account of a 'vagrant' juvenile eagle being seen feeding. On investigation all the shepherd found was the remnants of a hare's carcase.

For Mr Wolski it had been an exciting but strange time. His pleasure at the escape had for some reason given way now to even more sadness in the presence of the eagles that were still caged, as if the escape of one had intensified the sense of imprisonment of the others. Yet he knew that most of them would never survive even if they were free and that most would probably want to stay where they had for so long been safe, secure and well fed.

The truth was that Mr Wolski was sad with himself, for he did not wish to stay on at the Zoo any longer. But there was nowhere else for him to go and anyway he had, one night, two years before, made a promise to stay on until his old friend the female golden eagle 'went free', which to him really meant until she died. But sometimes he had to laugh at this, for if anything she seemed stronger than ever and it was beginning to look as if she might outlast him.

Yet it was a strange and contradictory fact that on those grim days when even the May blossom and the busy life of all the creatures around the Park could not shake off the ever present fact of the bars and cages of the Zoo and the imprisoned animals, Mr Wolski found silent comfort in the presence of the remaining golden eagle. She seemed calm and peaceful, and a few minutes in her presence soon cheered Mr Wolski up.

*

If ever afterwards Creggan had been asked at what moment on that journey north he knew he was free he would have been able to answer precisely. After the Southern Uplands of Scotland he had had to pass near to another industrial city and one quite as grim and dark as the others he had seen. But this one was different.

Beyond it, and quite easily seen, lay massive uplands and long and beautiful lochs with a glow of late spring light and majesty of bracken-covered sides that rose higher, and higher and yet higher into misty moorlands that brought an awe to his heart.

The moment came when, with the warmth of clear sunlight rising from the east, these mists cleared and he saw before him an upland range that dwarfed all others he had seen. Glen after great glen, river after loch, bracken slope after forested range, all without the sight or sound of Man. A wilderness in which an eagle could stretch his wings over ground that red deer, wild cat and blue mountain hare might roam. It was the magnificent beginnings of the mountains and moorlands of the Grampian range, and seeing it before him, Creggan knew that his dream to reach Cape Wrath once more might after all come true.

There was something about this huge expanse of rugged land that changed his sense of time. Urgency went from his wing-beats, the course he had set from the Park so many weeks before now weakened and drifted. He had things to learn before he finally pushed for home.

But first, he had to meet his own kind.

That they were near he had no doubt, for here and there he saw remnant nests and one evening, from out of some bleak crags, three hooded crows flew up at him, black, grey, sinister. Woil had told him that where they flew golden eagles would be near.

His reaction on seeing them was a surprise to himself, and a shock to them. He soared higher to lure them up and then folding his wings back stooped down towards them, gaining speed with each second and transfixing the weakest-looking one with his stare. Perhaps the hooded crows thought it was a game, perhaps they misjudged his skill and speed. However it was, the one he had aimed at did not get out of the way in time and a last-minute attempt to slink off in the wind failed. Creggan thumped straight into him at speed, the sound of it travelling across the glen. As the crow fell dead out of the sky into rough pine forest far below the other two turned to flee, calling out in alarm. Creggan could not turn fast enough to catch them before they dropped untidily into the safety of the trees below. But he planed over the pine trees calling out powerfully, the sound of it echoing among the heather-clad pools of the moor, and into the recesses of the silent pine forest. He wanted to announce that he commanded these skies.

But if that was what he believed, it was not true. For while Creggan had been attacking the hooded crow he had been watched and now he in his turn was being stooped upon. The first he knew of it was a warning call from high above where he saw the angry silhouette of a golden eagle stooping. The next he knew there was a shape in the sky to his left, moving fast towards him a little from below. He could neither move to attack nor take evasive action.

They came on him rapidly and powerfully and he decided that all he could do was to circle in a gentle way to indicate that he was not hostile, his heart filled with joy to see his own kind.

Their calls came ahead of them.

'Your name?'

'Your destination?'

'Your intent?'

'Now answer us!'

There was a strength and hardness about their voices that took away the pride he had felt at disposing of the hooded crow so effectively. The lower one, male, came first and circled round and round Creggan, staring at him and asking 'Your name? Your name?' so fast that Creggan had to circle to keep him in sight, and could not keep a clear eye on the other one approaching from above.

She came between them at speed, the air thunderous in her wings, which were more massive than any golden eagle's he had yet seen or imagined. There was a health and vigour about them both that made him feel weak again, and intimidated.

'I am glad to see you . . .' he began.

'Get on with it, stranger,' said the male.

'My name is Creggan. I am from the South . . .'

'You speak with a strange accent I have not heard before. Which part are you from?'

'The far South.'

'There aren't any eagles there,' said the female. 'Attack him,' she commanded her mate.

'No . . . no,' said Creggan quickly, 'I mean no harm. I just wanted . . .'

'What you want is no concern of ours. Attack him,' said the female again, circling above them both.

'But I . . .' and then the male turned in the air and presented his talons viciously towards Creggan.

Anger and courage came to him.

'I am a golden eagle,' he said fiercely, 'and I mean no harm to you or yours.'

'He speaks with pride,' said the female.

'He killed the hooded crow with skill,' said the male.

'Where are you from?' asked the female again.

'I . . .' and Creggan knew that they would not understand the truth if he tried to explain it. These eagles would not know what a zoo was, or believe that he had escaped from one in a place where no eagles lived naturally.

'Once, a long time ago, I was of Wrath in the far north-west. That is where I am from.'

At this the female looked both amused and angry.

'Wrath! Well, you certainly don't look like it. You look like a vagrant to me, and a pathetic one too even if you have learnt to kill crows. Wrath!' And with that she turned on him herself and raising up her wings struck him such a blow with her talons that he rolled back out of control in the air, the tops of the pine trees below spinning before his eyes.

They circled above him menacingly, the female laughing as he struggled to regain the line of his flight.

'I wouldn't let an eagle of Wrath hear you claim that!' she said. 'For they are a proud and fierce race and would kill any that claimed to be their kin who was not.'

'Not that there are many left now in any case from what I've heard,' said the male.

The female laughed again and nodded.

'Most have been exterminated, and good riddance to them. Proud vicious lot they were.'

'Now, *you*,' said the male, 'you'd better get going, and fast. Go back to the west coast where you probably came from and join the other vagrants there. Skulk along the shore and feed off others' carrion. Learn to fly. Learn to fight. And when you have, you had better avoid our territory, for we do not like weak eagles who hide behind the names of once-proud families like Wrath.'

The anger that had been in Creggan left him. And so too did the fear. Minch had taught him that neither feeling was useful to an eagle unless it was controlled. He found that strong though they were, and better in the air, this pair of eagles did not frighten him now.

He would leave but he would not forget.

Very quietly he said with a pride and authority that seemed to surprise them, 'I *am* of Wrath and have much to learn. But the time will come when my race will be proud of me. What is the name of this territory.'

'Rannoch,' said the male. 'Now get going fast.'

'I will not forget that name,' said Creggan coldly.

Then, with as much dignity as he could find, which lay more in his spirit than anything else for he was still shaken by the buffeting the female had given him, he turned west and left them.

'Wrath!' he heard the female say.

'I'm glad he wasn't,' said the male, 'or else we might have had trouble.'

Which brought pride back into Creggan's heart even though he was driven away, and made him even more determined to bring honour to the name of Wrath.

13

Creggan's arrival among his own kind in Scotland coincided with the breeding season and he was not welcome by the pairs whose territory he crossed.

Minch had long ago taught him the rule among eagles that unless an eagle is seeking to take over territory then he should leave a pair to rear their young in peace.

He drifted westward to the highland coast and then only slowly north for he was in no hurry to get to Wrath. His encounters with the eagles he met convinced him that he was not yet experienced or powerful enough to seek territory of his own, or to head for the far north-west where golden eagles are notoriously fierce and strong.

He had desired to go to his homesite just once, not because he expected his parents to greet him with pleasure – he knew they would long ago have forgotten him in the act of rearing many other young even if they were still alive – but because it was there he had first been caught. He wanted to go there once more and start out again, choosing his own route and finding his own freedom. He wanted, too, to fly out over Cape Wrath itself, and feel the sea-winds rise under his wings, for his father had said that only then could he truly call himself an eagle of Wrath.

He was troubled by the strange things the Rannoch eagles had said about the Wrath eagles being exterminated and wondered if his own capture had been part of that. If they had been, then his own parents and the rest of his kind would now be gone and the territory might be free. But he knew it was more likely that alien golden eagles would have taken it

over and it might not be easy to win it back for his own. So
Creggan was in no hurry.

Around him he began to see the unfolding beauty of early
summer in his homeland and it held him still with wonder
and made him forget the passing of the days.

He saw the bleak and unpromising moorland gain colour
as the grasses grew and the flowers came. The pink petals of
moss campion on highland wastes, the whites and pinks of
saxifrage among the scree and rock beneath great cliffs; while
in more sheltered spots, where streams ran, he found mosses
whose greens were bright with life, and ferns whose intricate
leaves moved quietly with the breeze.

Along the western coast, on the shores of island, rock and
cliff he saw cushions of pink sea thrift on rocks where lichens
of yellow and red and green made each ancient rock a beauty
in itself. For long solitary hours he would take stance on some
sea cliff watching the sharp-winged flutter of terns as they
hung above the sea to fish, or the magnificent splashes of
great gannets, or the rugged gliding of herring gulls.

It was a time to think and to watch, and a time to learn. His
skill at hunting living prey increased each day until he could
stoop on a hare from half a mile away, judging its path and
speeding his attack so that he hit it with such force that it
was dead before his talons fully closed on it. Sometimes too
he would take duck and geese as they floated on some high
lochan, coming on them so low along the ground that they
only saw him when the massive darkness of his wings came
over the peat edge and shadowed out their life.

Sometimes he would secretly watch other eagles whose
territory he had trespassed over, to learn from them the art
of quartering back and forth over an area to find prey and
flush it out.

He also learned all he could of the ground and the way it
shaped the wind, because command of the wind meant
command of flight and that meant dominance and security.

Occasionally he met other vagrants like himself, but most

were unfriendly and only anxious to establish their power and strength. A few would talk and from them he learned what he could of the north-west. One confirmed that the Wrath eagles had been exterminated and that eagles of grim Caithness had infiltrated westward. Another revealed that the last of the Callanish eagles was gone for 'that place too has been taken over by Men who put to death what eagles they find. Only a few linger on, but the old Callanish eagles are no more and will never come back.'

But Minch had often told him that faith in Callanish waxed and waned through time as the wind itself changes through the day, and that eagles often forgot it, and wanted to forget. 'There will come a time, Creggan, when you will learn that the fretting here in these Cages when you think the world has passed you by has taught you more than all the flights, and kills, and territories you may have made or seen. Here you have learnt the lore, and learnt to feel those powers other eagles forget.'

Creggan had learnt by now not to talk of his past, or to try and explain about the Zoo he had escaped from. Even to him it was now barely imaginable, and other eagles he mentioned it to seemed to take it as a lie and untruth, and were angry at him for trying to delude them. As for coming from Wrath, well, any eagle could tell from his accent and flight that he was not a north-west eagle. So he would be vague, and talk of the south, and say he had been a vagrant for many years. Which in a way was true.

The months passed and there came a week when the purple flowers of the heather took over the moorland slopes and brought with it the sense at last of autumn, a time he loved.

The young of that year were beginning to leave their home territories, pairs were beginning to relax and there was a sense of change in the air again. It was then that he felt his true strength as an eagle coming at last. He began to notice that those juveniles who were on his line of flight deferred to him, preferring to back off rather than confront him. At first he was surprised at this and only when they referred to him as an 'adult' did he realize that some time in the previous weeks the last of his juvenile plumage had moulted and his wings now had the rich and glossy glow of an adult golden eagle.

He knew the time had come to head directly north along the western coast and investigate Cape Wrath at last.

As he travelled, so the last of the migrations travelled south past him – the arctic tern, the redwing, and some of the gulls. The heads of the black-headed gulls were turning white now, and on the moorland the fur of the mountain hares was already moulting into white for the winter.

From the west and north powerful gales swept from off the north Atlantic Ocean, sending great waves roaring into the cliffs below his flight, and spumes of sea-spray came up to put salt on his wings.

The islands that had seemed green and pink and blue in the summer now became distant grey rocks lost in rough seas that sent the flotsam and jetsam of man and nature high upon the stormridden shores.

Although Creggan preferred in such weather to keep inland he had a natural preference for the coast and on calmer days when the wind abated he would spend a few hours along the shore. Sometimes there was sea carrion to find there, or injured sea birds.

One day as dusk was falling and he was feeding in a deserted cove at a dead razorbill he had found, and a heavy grey sea rolled in among the great rocks below the high-tide mark, Creggan became aware that he was being watched. Man? Creature? He did not know. The wind was blowing from the sea and he instinctively opened his wings, leaned round into it and circled up and back, quartering the cliffs around him with his eyes to see what or who was there.

The light was bad and only shadows among sheer rock greeted him, and the occasional fulmar gliding stiffly across the cliff face. He continued circling upwards and then cut away from the cove, flying over the moorland gloom before turning sharply back to observe the cove again. He flew low back to the highest part of the cliff overlooking the cove and took stance to see what appeared.

Time passed and the afternoon light began to fade and Creggan was just beginning to think that he might go back to the carrion he had found before the incoming tide took it, when he saw movement from shadows far below, and the opening of great wings. It was a young female golden eagle, and she was going for the carrion he had left. He decided then and there to take the carrion off her and have it back for himself and so leaned out into the void and tilted into the wind towards her far below.

But as he did he saw two hooded crows scutter along the cliff face and sneak down upon her, calling threateningly, and as she turned to them he was astonished to see that she moved clumsily, uncertainly, not as an adult eagle should. He hovered and watched. She seemed to assess their position and then go quickly back to the carrion as if she was very hungry and sought to take as much of it as she could before the crows reached her.

The crows attacked and her movements were strangely slow and disorientated as if she could not quite see them, or make her wings and talons move as she intended. His anger at her taking his carrion was gone and instead focused on the miserable hooded crows. He pulled his wings back for speed, leaned into the wind to gain maximum drive and stooped down upon them, the air thunderous in his wings as, with talons thrust forward, he thumped the first straight to its death among the wet beach rocks and tore at the other viciously before it squawked and fled to safety in the shadows of the cliff.

Then he landed some distance off and stared at her. She said nothing, but hungrily returned to the carrion to take what more she could, as if she expected him to take the rest from her. She was strong of wing and yet had about her a frailty that suggested illness.

'What is your name and where are you from?' he asked formally.

'The islands,' she said as she took the prey. 'I come from there. Whoever you are I did not need your help.'

When she said this she looked full at him for the first time and ill though she seemed he saw in her eyes the full pride and command of an eagle.

'You looked weak to me,' he said. 'The hooded crows would have had your food.'

She stopped eating and fell silent looking at him. After a time she sighed and said, 'It is true enough. We vagrants have to seem strong when we may feel weak. It is the only way we can survive. Two days ago I ate baited carrion left out for fox or crow over in Skye and its effects were to poison me and make me feel near death. Yesterday I could barely fly. Today it has been worse and it is getting worse now. But I knew I must try to feed if I was to survive. I sheltered in this cove and saw you eating the carrion here and came to take it after you had gone.'

Then she added softly: 'I thank you for your help. It is a sorry thing when an eagle cannot even ward off two miserable hooded crows. I would normally have killed them with one strike of my talons!'

A heavier wave from the sea sent spray and water surging up towards them and they both lifted instinctively on the wind as the wave rushed under them. He saw she had difficulty doing it.

'I do not know if I even have strength enough to regain the shelter I have just come from . . .' and her wings seemed to weaken by the second and her eyes to be pained.

'Come,' said Creggan, 'I will lead you there.' And he half hopped and half flew up the rough beach, stopping frequently to see that she was following, until with a final struggle they got back to safe rocks along the cliffs over the tideline.

By some unspoken agreement they settled quietly together to watch the night fall and the heavy tide thunder in. As darkness came he could hear her laboured breathing and knew that she was as ill as she said.

Night fell and brought with it a high rolling tide and strong wind. Creggan could not rest or sleep, for out of the racing seas beneath their stance seemed to come troubled memories and images of a place where he once was, and eagles he once knew. Their wings were chained and across their grim faces fell metal bars and from behind them rose the howling of wolves and the terrible roaring of caged beasts.

He shivered and turned in the darkness towards his unknown companion.

'What is your name?' he asked.

'Faele,' she whispered, 'I am of the islands but a vagrant now like you . . .' She did not say more and when he came closer he saw that if it was sleep that had found her it was of a troubled nightmare kind, the sleep of the ill and the stressed. She groaned and seemed troubled. He stayed close, hoping his warmth might help her, staring protectively out into the night as if the strange images he saw might try to harm her. He remembered another night like this when an eagle he had known had been very ill and he had invoked the powers of Callanish. He found peace in the fact that this time he could help, and decided to watch over her until she recovered.

When morning came she was too ill with the poison to move and despite her weak protests he told her he would watch over her, for no eagle should be prey to gull or crow. He left her for a time to find prey and brought back a hare from the moorland tops, tearing it up and gently feeding her with parts of it.

For two days he helped her and took stance at night near by, pleased to hear her breathing gradually ease and improve, and watching as she began to sleep in a less troubled way.

It was on the evening of the fourth day that she raised her wings and flexed them in the sea-wind. She turned to him and he saw her eyes were clear and out of pain.

'Why did you help me?' she asked. 'For surely vagrants like us prefer to pass each other by.'

'I could not see one of my own kind suffer,' he said, 'or leave her to be attacked by crows.'

'Where does your kindness come from?' she asked, and said it almost as if she expected no answer.

Creggan was silent for a long time.

Then he said, 'I knew an eagle once who was also ill and close to death. I could not help her directly but only invoke the greatest power we eagles have. She helped me as well and when I saw you were ill I did for you what she would have wanted me to do.'

'What a mysterious speech!' said Faele. 'An eagle you could not help . . . the greatest power we have . . . you were helped by her . . . Now tell me what is your name and where are you from, and who was the eagle you wanted to help?'

He laughed.

'Well, it seems to be the vagrants' code not to say where we come from or whither we are bound . . .'

' "Whither we are bound!" You do speak in a strange way, like the old eagles used to.' It was her turn to laugh. 'Where did you learn such an expression?'

Creggan hesitated to tell her but she seemed different from other vagrants he had met and in the last few days a trust had developed between them, so it seemed natural to say.

'My homesite was Cape Wrath but before I ever made my first flight a Man came and . . .' and he began to tell her his story, of the Zoo, of the Cages, of the Men there and his sudden escape . . . only leaving out mention of the other eagles in the Cages for in his heart he knew their pride would ask that he did not mention their names to a free eagle, nor would they wish for pity from outside.

Yet when he had finished the first thing she said was, 'But you haven't really talked of the most important thing – the other eagles who were with you. Was the one you mentioned who was ill one of them? Was it the Cages that prevented you helping her?'

Creggan nodded.

'Tell me of her,' she asked.

'She is proud and wise and speaks with authority of many things. There is peace in her wings and though she is old now yet she has a strength such as no eagle I have ever met has. She has learned from her suffering and believes always in the power of her homesite. She told me that eagles from there carry a great burden and for some it is hard.'

'Where is she from?' asked Faele.

'It is a site of which I have heard strange things since I came north,' said Creggan, 'where the eagles are in decline and their powers going. But I do not believe that for I have felt those powers. She came from Callanish.'

Faele was suddenly silent.

'What is her name?' she whispered.

But before Creggan could say it a look in her eyes stopped him and he waited. She stared out westward across the sea.

'You are strange to these parts though you were born near here, for Wrath is not so many miles to the north. Do you know where Callanish is?'

He shook his head.

'It is across this sea and in summer on a good day it is easy enough to see the island where the sacred site is. Do you know the name of this sea that we face?'

He shook his head again and her voice became a whisper.

'It is called the Minch.'

Creggan said nothing but stared over the grey rolling sea that had given the eagle whom he loved most in the world her name. At that moment he would have given up every moment of his past and future freedom to have her at his side.

'Is *her* name Minch?' asked Faele quietly.

Creggan nodded, for it seemed this eagle would know the truth of anything he said.

'And you say there is peace in her wings and wisdom in her heart.'

'Yes,' said Creggan, 'it is so.'

'And you say she said that eagles of Callanish carry a burden and that for some it is hard . . .' and her voice drifted into a distance.

'But what of you?' asked Creggan. 'What is your story?'

He could sense that she had travelled far as a vagrant and had seen much and that like him she was in some way returning home.

'Where is your homesite?' he asked.

Her head bent low.

'I was born in a place of shadows, of memories, of decline. Where we were told that we were not what our ancestors were. Men came. Many were killed as they were in Wrath. Others fled. Others left behind their faith in their home-sites . . .'

'But where are you from?'

She looked across the sea she had called the Minch. It rolled towards them and beyond it, grey and obscure on the horizon, rose a low island.

'It is the Isle of Lewis,' she whispered.

'But that's where . . .' but Creggan did not finish. She turned to him and stared into his eyes, and said, 'I am of Callanish. I come from where Minch came from. When you spoke of this eagle I knew whom you meant for she was the last of our kind who carried wisdom in her wings. My parents remembered her and often spoke of her, saying that her flight was as beautiful as an autumn sunset. But that was many years ago when they were still juveniles and one day she disappeared and none of the eagles there has since had the full power of a Callanish eagle.

'When I was young I dreamed of being like her. Then I became a vagrant and travelled far and nowhere; now I have come back to be near Callanish again, though quite where I shall go I don't know. It is a great burden to be a Callanish eagle and live at the site itself. I do not think I have the strength. But I have come north again to be near it . . .'

Then they stared at each other in silence and saw into each other's heart, sensing that each was a little afraid of what was to come, and of the powers that they felt were in their wings and across their lives and which had brought them together. Each knew without saying that the powers of Callanish would bind them and that whatever was to come would guide them.

'I am northward bound for Cape Wrath,' said Creggan purposefully, 'and will find territory there and make it mine. Will you come?'

Faele came closer to him.

'I think that the powers of Callanish have been guiding me to Wrath all my life,' she said. Then she added with a light laugh, 'I do not think, Creggan, that you could stop me.'

They waited for two more days until Faele had recovered her strength and the winds had quietened. Then they soared into the sky as one, to make flight north as a pair along the coast to Wrath.

14

It was April six months later and the mountains and moorlands of Wrath stretched silent and pure beneath a layer of thick snow. Here and there on higher ground a crack of black rock stood out against the white; while in the glens the flat surface of icy lochans reflected a pale blue sky.

No sound, but for the whisper of wind over the surface of snow, and the occasional harsh call of unseen ptarmigan across the vast waste.

Near the centre of the great square of territory that makes up Wrath, inaccessible from road or coast, rises a mountain. Its name is Creag Riabhach and its steepest side faces northeast and from its top, on a clear day, the sea can be seen to west, to east, to north.

Above the Creag, circling on the air currents there, two eagles soared together: Creggan and his mate Faele.

'This is the place where we can make a site,' he was saying.

But Faele was uncertain still, as she had been for days.

They had finally come to Wrath in the deep winter and found it devoid of eagles except for a few vagrants half-heartedly trying to establish territory. The only opposition they faced was from some slant-eyed Caithness infiltrators who came up from the south-east mountains soon after their arrival and challenged them.

Creggan turned so boldly upon them, and Faele followed the pattern of his flight so confidently, that the Caithness eagles simpered and whispered before them, and made their retreat.

'You can have it,' they hissed as they left. 'We never really wanted it anyway. It's a miserable place where Men roam and kill eagles.'

Then seeing that this comment did not please Creggan they added in a conciliatory way, 'But we golden eagles should not fight. Where are you from?'

Although the Caithness eagles tried to sound confident and calm they were in fact afraid, for never had they seen such a certain pair as these two who cast their great shadows over the ancient territory of Wrath as if they had occupied it for many long seasons.

'My name is Creggan and I was born of Wrath and it gives me no pleasure to see your shadows cross my homesite. So leave now, and return only in peace.'

With these bold words Creggan advanced upon them with Faele circling above him, and the Caithness eagles slipped thankfully away.

After that they decided to establish their territory with flights of power along its boundaries under the winter skies so that all who might see, whether vagrant eagle, or hunting falcon, or buzzard or raven or hooded crow, would know whose territory it was.

Until finally they came to its most northerly part where the east and west coastlines of Britain meet as one to face out on to the Atlantic wastes as Cape Wrath. Above these great cliffs they flew a pairing flight such that all who saw it would not forget their strength and joint purpose.

So did Creggan and Faele take their territory.

Now, according to the ancient rite of pairs, Creggan sought out different sites to raise young and Faele judged them, using her skill to decide which of those that Creggan liked would most suit her.

Of them all he favoured the centrally placed mass of Creag Riabhach and it was above this that he now soared, anxiously watching as she cut back and forth below him assessing the site. He had shown her others – two along the western cliffs, and his own homesite on the mountain of Fashven which overlooked Loch Airigh na Beinne which he dimly remembered as a juvenile. It was from there he had been taken by Man but she dismissed the site as being too near a road, which now, in the white snow, they could see as a thin unnatural shadowed line across the landscape.

Creag Riabhach was further off and hard to reach except by flight and it had a commanding view over moor, and loch, and distant Cape.

Its north-east face was too steep to hold snow, but ice hung in its sheer crevices and far below, where the ground levelled off, the snow had been dirtied by black scatters of rockfall from the cliff.

Creggan could tell by the slowness of Faele's flight along the cliff face, and the way she carefully examined the Creag and the approaches to it that she was excited by it.

'The aspect this side is good,' she called out, 'it faces north-east and will protect our young from the direct sun; while below lies what may be the best of the hunting-grounds through the summer months.'

'From the top you can see danger for miles around,' cried out Creggan, adding as a pleasant afterthought, 'and there is a sense of sea in the air.'

Above them both the sky lightened into blue, while below the winter sun shone upon the snow, sending runnels of thawed water down the great cliff face. Near its top was the perfect nesting site, a place in shadow but overlooking the glens and lochs now filled with sun; a place to see and not be seen with the cliff hollowed into a recess which was overhung from above and sheer below.

'Here!' cried out Faele, 'This is the place.'

She took stance there briefly, and then leaned out into the void before her, opened her great wings and gyred up towards Creggan. Though the wind was light yet they found sufficient lift from it to soar ever higher, and turn over in the sky in their joy and tumble at each other above a spinning world, to make a display across the sky of wings that would wrest from Wrath's bleakness a summer of life and young.

How busy they were in the weeks of spring that followed as the snow melted and they fetched and carried what branches and vegetation and smaller driftwood they could find to build an eyrie. There were some bleached sticks upon a site a little way along the Creag they occupied, perhaps the nest of one of Creggan's ancestors, so they transported these to their new site. The heather and grass below the cliff sprang back to life almost as they watched and they became a part of the eternal cycle of life that caged eagles never know. It filled the moors with its sights and sounds. The ptarmigan moulted their white winter plumage and when the snows had gone the males started to mark out their territories, their harsh aggressive cries coming up to where Creggan and Faele looked over the scene.

Creggan quartered the moor and coast for food. Often he found some sticks on the distant shore to add to the nest and would labour with them for miles over the moor to the site; at the end of May he came upon a mountain ash in a river gully, its young leaves green with life, and tearing a branch off he took it back to the eyrie to twine around its rim.

Red deer slowly moved up from the south in small herds and sheep from the lower glens. While along the coast the sudden flutings of oystercatchers and haunting calls of curlews began to break the long winter's bleakness, as gull and tern cut across the cliffside winds.

There came a day in May when Faele stayed for a long time on the nest, patterning the soft woodrush that Creggan had brought into a nesting cup at the centre of the nest. And there, two days later, the first of a pair of eggs showed.

Now Creggan was filled with strength and purpose, and began the incessant hunting and returning to the nest with prey which would let Faele stay still until a chick was hatched.

They rarely saw Men across the moor though on the distant road to the north a car might occasionally travel. While at

night, from the distant Cape, a light would flash from the tall
tower Men had built there, its rhythmic beam soon becoming
a familiar thing they grew to like.

The warmth of early summer came and Faele stayed
always on the nest until at last, in June, a chick was hatched,
a tiny downy frail thing that poked its timid face from under
Faele's wing and stared out on a huge and alien world. It
was a male, who from the moment his life began called out
his urgent need for food. He watched his father's great
wings vast and dark in the sky above as Creggan flew off to
find him food.

Faele would take prey from Creggan and tear it into tiny
parts for the chick, bending tenderly to its tiny beak in
response to its demands. The second egg never hatched and
after a time Faele rolled it out of the nest and watched it
smash itself on the scree far below.

Now Creggan, with two mouths to feed apart from his own,
found there was never enough time. The weeks passed
quickly and the chick grew fast and shed its early down as
proper darker eagle feathers formed and its face took on a
fierce proud look as its eyes began to see the world beyond
the nest.

Both watched and guarded well. If buzzard, gull or hooded
crow came near they mantled up and threatened with harsh
calls and soon their young did the same, raising his slight
wings in pathetic semblance of what his parents did, and
hissing out a warning at some unsuspecting hooded crow in
the distance, a warning that was lost on the mountain wind.

They called him Creag after the place where he was born,
and for its similarity to his father's name.

So did Creggan in his turn come to turn again the cycle of
life that had made him and to learn of the joys that Minch
had spoken of. He saw the work, the pain, the joy and love as
it came, and understood how Minch found pleasure in
watching other creatures outside the Cages making life. For
a time he found a peace in this.

So busy had they been that it was not until August, when Creag was nearly ready for flight, that they began to leave the nest for longer periods and have time alone together. It was then that Faele felt able to talk of Callanish and tell of the years of wandering she had had since she flew from it as a juvenile. She described the Stones there and told Creggan the legend Minch had already told him. She explained that in each generation only one or two of the eagles on those islands had the strength and wisdom to be truly called eagles of Callanish.

'I learnt much from my mother who was a Callanish eagle but it was a burden too great for me. And anyway, I was told that it was right to leave and wander for a while and learn what I could. The wisdom of Callanish is born of all golden eagles, not just the few who live there. It waxes and wanes like the moon or like the northern lights; it comes and it goes and comes back again. There are always those who say it is dying and then, just when they seem to be right it comes back again.

'But it is carried only in the wings of a very few and surely Minch is one of these. It is an honour for any eagle to help and support such eagles.'

'Even if it means risking life, and territory?' asked Creggan quietly.

'Yes,' said Faele, fearing much that he should say that.

'I can never forget that I made a vow that she would escape even before me,' said Creggan, 'and yet she is still there and I am free. I can never rest easy here, or enjoy the many things I now have, so long as she is caged.'

Faele understood very well what Creggan was saying and yet she did not hesitate even though it might mean she would lose him for ever.

'That vow you made so long ago in the cage you escaped from; it invoked the powers of Callanish. The same powers gave you the cunning and courage to fly north and learn to be an eagle in the wild; they were the destiny that made us meet. If you feel them in you again I cannot stop you following them, and if I did we would never be happy.'

Creggan was looking across the moor at the patterns the shadows of the clouds made as they drifted south. One came slowly across the stance they had taken and the warmth of the sunlight faded to a sudden shiver of cold.

He was thinking of Faele's belief in Callanish and the faith she must have that those powers should be followed, whatever the danger. He wished he did not feel afraid, for something that meant danger was calling to him from a great distance and though he did not want to hear it yet its call was becoming louder and more insistent.

'Creggan . . . Creggan . . .'

It was Faele's voice that interrupted his thoughts asking what the matter was, and yet it seemed another eagle calling and one that needed him and whose call he must find the courage to answer.

'Creggan . . . Creggan, what is it that troubles you?' Faele asked. But he could only shake his head and say it was nothing but the shadow of a passing cloud.

It was soon after that that Creag made his first flight, his wings opening nervously over the great cliff at the edge of the eyrie for hour after hour before he gained courage enough to fly.

But Creggan gained no pride from it. He surveyed his territory, his Faele, his son in flight and the distant sea, but felt that though he had never wished for more than he had now yet the joy it gave him was shadowed by the sense that his duty lay elsewhere. It was as if he was still in a cage except that here the bars were invisible and of his own making.

September, October . . . and with the first cold mists of winter the red deer disappeared south as the hare and ptarmigan began their moult into white for the winter. The purple of the heather faded; rain swept where sun had been;

the smooth loch ruffled into wavelets before the strong winter winds.

A grim silence came upon Creggan and he spent many days and nights alone, wandering the coastline of Wrath seeking something he could not find. Sometimes he would see Creag on the skyline and take him food, for he still had to learn to hunt effectively. Sometimes he saw Faele and hid away from her, for he felt he had nothing to say.

Until at last she flew to him and asked him again to tell her what it was that troubled him.

'It is a calling, a fretting which will not leave me still. I know what I have here is everything I want and yet now that we are less busy and have time to think I am troubled.'

'By what?'

'By that vow I made before the powers of Callanish.'

She listened and was troubled. She felt a terrible fear for she sensed that he might never be free in his heart of those years in the Zoo.

'Go to Callanish,' she said at last. 'Fly there to the sacred site and listen to the wind among the stones. They will guide you and set you free.'

'That is what Slorne the tawny eagle said as I escaped . . .' remembered Creggan. ' "Trust those powers that have brought you this chance, trust your strength . . . these things will guide you." That was what she said.'

'She was right. Leave me here with Creag, who needs time yet to grow strong enough to leave the territory. He will be safe enough and will find his wings faster in your absence. Fly to Callanish, my love . . .'

'Slorne told me one other thing,' said Creggan. 'Her last words to me as I flew up into the night were "Send us a sign . . ." What do you think she meant by that? What sign?'

'Perhaps she meant that she wanted to know that you were truly free so that she and the others could be at peace in the knowledge that all their hopes were carried in your wings.'

Creggan was silent then and understood the wisdom she

must have to understand these things, and the courage she needed to tell him to fly off to Callanish.

'Well,' he said at last, 'I will go.'

But first Creggan flew to his son Creag and made a flight with him over their homesite to tell him to protect Faele for 'the next few days' while he was gone, and act as an adult male eagle should in guarding the territory.

Then, when he was satisfied that Creag would do so, Creggan made a last farewell to Faele and turned from Wrath to fly west over the open sea to Callanish. He immediately felt happier to be answering the call he had been denying so long with action and flight.

But as Wrath disappeared behind him under grey November skies and the isle on which Callanish lay loomed on the horizon, his desire to fly there weakened.

He hung over the sea hesitant and unsure. For the calling came not from Callanish but from the far south; it came not as whispers of wind among great Stones but as the cries for help from eagles who were his friends and were cast for ever in the Cages he remembered with such horror.

'Creggan . . . Creggan!' Their voices were a clamour of sound and entreaty in his mind and he knew he must answer them. So he turned south towards where the Men were, south where danger lay.

South; from where he might never find the strength or good fortune to escape again.

PART THREE

THE FINAL RETURN

15

Of all the kinds of courage an eagle may display the greatest is that which, knowing all the dangers he faces by taking a particular course of action, yet drives him on to risk them.

Creggan knew the dangers very well and with each reluctant wing-beat he saw, and heard, and smelt the evidence of them.

Roads. Smoke. Industrial sound. The shore with its lining of tar and filth. The towns with their rings of rubbish around them. The loch that was once beautiful and is now lined with Man dwellings. The glen that cannot hide its dam and power station. At first, after leaving the natural silence of his territory, Creggan was easily able to avoid these things by keeping to the wilder coasts and higher ground. But the further south he got the harder it became, until he could not seem to find a route that did not pass ominously near the sound and sight of Men.

What had seemed wilderness to him on his flight north now seemed tame and dangerous. Even the great backbone of the Pennines, which had given him his first taste of wilderness when he first reached it from the south, he saw now was scarred and marked by the lines of Man. Down its length was a great track and even in the blustering weather of November in which he now flew groups of people walked wearing bright unnatural colours. Good for an eagle to avoid, he thought to himself wryly; but better if an eagle wasn't going their way at all.

He was careful to use all the skills he had learned in hunting prey to avoid them seeing him, keeping low and using the shadows of cliffs to lurk by, and cutting over the horizon quickly and dipping out of sight again as soon as he could. But he knew that sooner or later he would be seen by Man.

His passage slowed. Each day, each hour, he hesitated to go on and yet found himself inexorably drawn south by a calling that he could not ignore.

'Creggan! Creggan!' it seemed to say. 'Come now, give us a sign, show as that for one of us at least these long years are over. Give us hope . . .' Then, when he found himself longing to turn back towards his homesite, his beloved Faele, and his firstborn son Creag, it seemed to him that the faces and wings of Kraal and Slorne were there beckoning, and old Minch who had given him so much.

So on he went, until at last the line of the Pennines petered out into lowland, and he knew the last lap of his grim journey would soon be over. And then what would he do, and what could he achieve?

*

Every year the British Trust for Ornithology records all reports of rare birds seen in unexpected places. Eagles especially are often 'seen' and BTO officials have got used to the fact that buzzards, which have a wide distribution along the Pennines and in the south, are mistaken for golden eagles, which have not.

But when a group of three BTO members, walking along the Pennine Way, reports seeing a golden eagle disturbed a mile off by a party of hill walkers wearing brightly coloured anoraks it is taken seriously.

A detailed description of the bird was made, and it was clearly an adult male golden eagle in exceptionally fine condition.

Three days later, and one hundred and twenty-five miles to the south the same bird was seen by two schoolboys, both experienced ringers of birds for the RSPB.

A day later, in the Oxfordshire village of Chadlington, it

was seen circling high over a field, and alighting briefly on top of a barn.

An item on BBC Oxford Radio announced the interesting news and by the next day the story was out: 'Return of the Eagle', announced the newspapers and in most the exciting possibility was raised that the eagle that had escaped from London Zoo nearly two years before was coming 'home'.

The news made Mr Wolski feel very strange. He had somehow grown more tired these last two years, not in body so much as spirit. His dislike for the Zoo had increased and yet something kept him there, something he could not understand. He told himself it was because he had no other job to go to and would lose the pension to which he was entitled if he stopped work early. And anyway, what could he do? Where could he go?

One reason why he had become more restless was because since the golden eagle escaped so dramatically some little part of him had escaped as well. He had decided then that he wanted to move out of London and find a little house of his own which he could decorate and put in order before he retired, though that was about eight years off yet. But he had saved money regularly each week from his wages and now he had quite a lot put by – enough, he thought, to buy a small house somewhere. But when he investigated it all he found that to be near enough to London to get to work would cost too much and then there would be the travelling and the fares on top of it. Anyway, it worked out that he would be paying much more in loans than in rent, which was fixed by the council in the little flat he had.

He had given up that idea only to find that the restlessness that inspired it stayed with him, and got worse.

Now as he went about his work around the Zoo, sweeping the paths and doing odd jobs, he could think of little else but the 'return' of the eagle. If it *was* the eagle that had escaped why had it come back? He felt that it was in some way a sign to him, a signal, but he did not know how to interpret it.

Then, one Sunday afternoon, on his day off, it was confirmed. London's Capital Radio was the first with the news. An eagle, *the* eagle probably, had been seen in the Park near the Zoo. It seemed peaceful and healthy and it had not moved nor approached the nearby Zoo. A reporter even gave a live broadcast, which Mr Wolski heard, describing it atop a plane tree in the Park. Later, said the announcer, they would be talking to a Keeper from London Zoo to see if the bird could be positively identified.

Mr Wolski did not wait for that. He decided that he was going to see for himself. It was a cold grey afternoon and so putting on a warm coat over his jacket he left his rooms to walk the half mile to Regent's Park.

He headed for a high point near the centre of the Park and from there saw quite clearly where the eagle was. The bird itself was out of sight but there was a trail of reporters, Park officials and TV technicians heading for a place where several people were already gathered and though the eagle was out of clear view at the top of a great oak it was so big, and the yellow and black of its feet so distinct that there was no doubt what it was.

Mr Wolski joined the gaggle of people gathered round. They were talking about it, and photographers were getting ready to take pictures the moment the eagle showed any sign of movement.

Mr Wolski stood there for over an hour as the evening darkened and the winds, mild for November, rattled at the few persistent leaves still on the tree and the eagle shifted occasionally about, revealing, to those watching far below, a quick profile of beak and head before it moved again and the great round edge of the wing and furrowed back hid its head again.

'I thought eagles flew!' said one of the newsmen after a time to another. Mr Wolski smiled.

'No, no, they sit for long periods doing nothing,' he said, looking at them for a moment, and then up at the eagle again.

'Do you know anything about eagles?' asked one of the reporters.

'Something. A little. I work in the Zoo.'

The faces of the two reporters changed from bored and getting cold to interested and getting warm. They began to look as if they might have struck gold.

'London Zoo?'

Mr Wolski nodded.

'You mean you know the eagles there?'

Mr Wolski smiled. 'I should do. I have worked there since after the Second World War.'

So Mr Wolski told them what he knew without realizing that they might print what he said. He would not attempt to recognize this bird but it seemed the same as he remembered, except it looked a lot more healthy to him. When they asked him what he felt about the birds being in captivity he said, 'I do not like it. Nobody knows if they *feel* anything as we do but I do not think a creature that is made to fly in the sky can be happy being confined for years in a cage that is no bigger than a council-house lounge, though a little taller. It does not seem natural to me.'

And Mr Wolski might have continued had not various Zoo officials appeared at that moment, including the Keeper, making him feel it was best if he left. He did not want to be involved in the recapture of this eagle. As he started to leave one of the reporters said, 'What's your name?' And when he told them 'Mr Wolski' they wanted to know his other name and he told them that too, 'Helmut'.

He made instinctively for the Zoo and when he was half-way there he stopped, turned and looked back. It was an ordinary grey November evening, though not so cold that he needed to button up his coat. But he could feel something extraordinary in the air, something to do with him and the eagles. He stared at the black shape at the top of the tree beneath which so many people had gathered and he somehow knew, seconds before it did so, that the eagle was going to fly. Sure enough, as if at a signal, it took off into the evening light, leaning forward and pushing so heavily that the whole of the top of the tree swayed at its departure.

There was an audible sigh of awe from the people gathered below as the eagle's great wings opened into magnificent silhouette against the sky and it swept over their heads towards the Zoo. Mr Wolski watched it coming, the sky seeming to be in its grasp and the Park to grow small before its flight, and it soared over his head and he watched it glide on towards the distant Cages whose stark shapes could be seen by the Park side of the Zoo.

Then he sighed and walked the way it had gone towards the Zoo. He knew that whatever was happening, whatever powers were in its flight and in its extraordinary return, was part of that strange uneasy change that had started on that distant night when he had stood at his bedroom window and made a vow.

In a way too he knew that the eagle was bringing freedom, and it was what he himself had dreamt of when he was a prisoner during the war. A freedom he thought he might find if, and when, he was released from captivity. But it had eluded him all these long years. Until now when, as he sensed in that lone eagle's flight, that freedom might at last be very near.

*

For days Minch had been restless and sad. The Men had been wary, watchful, careful, and there was in the shape of the clouds and the run of the winds a sense of change.

Kraal was worried about her because her mind seemed sometimes to wander and her speech to be strange.

'Callanish is calling now, Kraal, can you not hear it and see it in the sky?' she would say.

'These long years . . . nearly over now. Nearly at an end. Feel no anger, do not blame the Men. The power is not theirs to do or undo, nor ours.'

'What power, Minch? What is nearly over now?'

But she did not seem to hear him and only shook her faded old wings at the bars and bowed her head as if all around her, the eagles, the Men, the sky and the wind were, after all, nothing very much at all. And she, in a way, was even less.

What Kraal understood least of all was her acceptance of captivity.

'Don't you want to get out, Minch? Don't you still feel the anger you drove into me all through the years, reminding me of my home, asking me questions I did not want to answer? Did not your will somehow bring about the escape of Creggan, gone nearly two years now?'

'When you are young like Creggan, freedom seems outside beyond the Cages. But when you get older like me you find it is inside. He was too young to know that but he will learn it. I fear for him when he does.'

'Do you think he survived, Minch?' asked Woil quietly, for though he rarely said much he was listening. And the Chilean eagle who had taken Creggan's cage looked at her too. Like the rest of them he wanted to know the answer to that.

Minch stared out at the November evening.

Her wings ruffled. Her talons tensed and untensed. Her eyes could not settle. *Was* he alive?

For days she had asked that question and felt the answer coming nearer. For days she had felt the power of Callanish telling her to call, call out on the wind, northward where her homeland was. Restless, waiting, wondering, hoping. A hope that through all the years she had never dared *feel*, though she had expressed it often enough; a hope she thought had gone when she so nearly died.

'Somewhere near,' she whispered, 'he is alive. And in his wings he carries memories of us. His freedom is our freedom and each moment he lives for us . . .'

'What do you mean, he's *near*?' asked Kraal. 'How can he be near us here?'

But Minch ignored this and turned instead to Woil.

'Does he think of us sometimes?' whispered Woil, as if the thought that a free flying eagle might think of him, who was nothing and was lost for ever in the Cages, meant that somewhere in that great sky a tiny part of himself flew free.

'He will feel us thinking and hoping for his survival. He will never forget us . . .' But she let the words fade from her for she could feel him near her, her Creggan, whom she had given a strength and courage he would always have. As the dark of the evening fell she went close to the bars of her cage with the others listening and began to whisper, 'he is there, for Callanish is in him and he will send us a sign, a sign . . .'

At which Slorne opened her wings as if she understood the real meaning behind Minch's words and she stared out as Minch did into the evening light in front of the Cages. And the others sensed their awe and came to stare as well, for things were strange across the Zoo, strangely silent. They saw by the lights along the paths that there were Men standing about in silence, ominously waiting, as if they knew what Minch knew and that something was coming. They were all silent, all still, everything waiting.

Then high above those lights a shadow came, the pull of a great wing, the stare of an eye; the power of an eagle's glide.

'He is near us,' whispered Minch, 'he is near us. May Callanish protect him.'

At which words the sky in front of the Cages seemed to open, the darkness to become light, and the emptiness between the waiting Men and eagles to be filled as Creggan returned.

His great wings were bright with strength and health in the light of the lamps; his eyes clear. He flew free, and in freedom he came back, landing on one of the benches opposite the Cages and turning towards them.

He looked only at Minch, into her ancient wise eyes and she saw that he was older now and troubled, and that in his heart he was still caged and was not free.

'Go, Creggan, now that you have shown that you have

survived,' whispered Minch urgently. 'Go free before the Men come. Go for you can do no more for us. You owe us nothing, so go now.'

But Creggan said and did nothing. Only shook his head and stared round fearlessly as the Men slowly approached like great Stones out of the night.

And all the eagles watched in silence as the Men came and caged him once more.

16

'Why? Why did you come back and let them catch you?'

But Creggan could not tell them, however many times they asked.

'I just had to,' was all he could say. 'I was driven to come back by . . . a calling.'

'A *what*?' said Kraal. 'That just doesn't make sense!'

But Creggan could not say and could only stare away into the distant sky which was his domain no longer.

The Men had moved the Chilean eagle and put Creggan back in his original cage. He had watched them come to take him, he had felt their hands on him, he had seemed to see himself being moved into the cage and the door locked on him, as if it was a dream happening to another eagle.

But now it was not a dream but reality: the drab and stained concrete floor; the same dead branch, the bars, the fetid smells of the Zoo; the pathetic unnaturalness of Three Island Pond. The desperate boredom that will drive a creature mad.

'Why did I do it, Minch, why?'

Creggan had finished telling them his tale, of how he journeyed north and of all the things he had done; of Wrath, of Faele and of his firstborn, Creag. How closely they had all listened, how much joy they had found in his exploits. How aggressive Kraal had become when Creggan spoke of how the Rannoch eagles had attacked him on his arrival in Scotland.

'I would have gone for them, Creggan, I can tell you.

Attacking you when they should have been welcoming and given you honour!'

How peaceful Slorne had become when Creggan described the great beauty of his moorland home, and the flight of his beloved Faele across that ancient place.

How possessed old Minch seemed when he told her that Faele came from Callanish and remembered her name, and spoke of her as an honoured ancestor whom they all thought had died long ago.

And Woil, how strangely relieved he was when Creggan described the initial terror of flying into the sky outside the Cages, and how he had come to understand why Woil had been frozen with fear when he made his escape.

But these memories and consolations did not outweigh by one millionth part the tragedy of Creggan's return and capture; and now, when all was quiet and the first night back had set in, he turned to Minch to ask her if her wisdom could explain the reason for his coming back.

'What can I do here? What power do I have?' These things he asked again and again.

'Do you remember when you first came to the Cages?' asked Minch gently. 'So many years ago now it seems, and you came to replace me. Do you remember?'

'You were ill and seemed so old. I was even afraid of your voice.'

'Do you feel fear now?' asked Minch.

Creggan shook his head.

'Nor *am* I ill. Your coming saved my life, your faith then in the fact that I was of Callanish gave me strength as it has so many times since, even though then, when you first told Kraal I would survive, you did not even know the lore of Callanish.

'Well now, Creggan, you have come back and *I* have to ask the reason why, not you. I have felt your coming for many weeks now, and felt that something would happen. For you made a vow that if ever the chance came I would go free before you and . . .'

'But how do you know? Did Slorne speak and tell you?'

Minch shook her head.

'No, she never spoke of it. But I felt that vow, and I saw your reluctance to leave and in a way I was glad. Rightly or wrongly we here are your family, we are your memory, we are what you will pass on in word and action to your young; to Creag and to Faele who shared your territory with you.'

' "Will"!' said Creggan bitterly. 'Not any more. I will never see them again.'

'Listen to the night as it falls, listen to the sounds that I have begun to hear when others are asleep, listen to the wind in the trees . . . can you hear it?'

Above them a light wind whispered in the branches of the plane trees, now soft, now loud, now faint, now strong.

'Listen . . . and tell me what you hear.'

'It is like the distant sea on a quiet night in the eyrie that Faele and I built. Rushing up the beaches and against the rocks, running to the cliffs and rippling over sand.'

'Listen, Creggan, and think of Callanish, where the wind whispers and the sea breaks, the one over heather and the other over rock . . . listen . . .'

And Creggan could hear the sea and it was near, and he heard the wind among great Stones, in a place to which he had begun to fly but which whispered to him to turn south, to fly south to his friends, to trust and have faith in that power that once made eagles and Men stand as one by the great Stones of Callanish.

*

And an old man listened to the sound of the sea, and the whisper of the wind, as he had listened for so many years; and he was restless. Slowing now with age, not much time left and so much to do.

He stood at the tiny window of his old croft in the Western

Isles of Scotland and stared over the marram grass into the pale night. November, but enough stars and glimmer from an old moon to see the stones of Callanish.

On the rough wooden table by the peat fire that was all the heat he had was a newspaper and it lay open at a centre page.

'THE FINAL RETURN' was the headline, and it showed the picture of a male eagle staring out of a cage in London Zoo. The story had made national headlines, and if he had had a television, which he did not, he would have seen it on the News. The extraordinary return of an eagle to a Zoo, because, said the keepers, 'he probably felt happier here, where he is safe, than out in the wild'. The old man shook his head and muttered 'No, no,' in a voice that was broken and rough with age. But it was not the young eagle that interested him so much as the old one in the cage next door to him who had been at the Zoo said the newspaper for 'over thirty years'.

He had another newspaper there as well, or rather a cutting from one, and it showed a Mr Wolski standing by the Cages with the old eagle behind him. The newspaper talked about Mr Wolski's connection with the eagle that 'went back thirty years to when the eagle first came to the Zoo "from somewhere in Scotland" '.

'From Callanish,' muttered the old man.

He read again, as he had read many times these last few days, the words of Mr Wolski – words for which this Mr Wolski had got into trouble with the Zoo authorities: 'I do not think a creature that is made to fly in the sky can be happy to be confined for years . . .' and the old man sat heavily at the table and nodded to himself muttering agreement with the thought.

Then he turned to the wooden mantelpiece behind him, beneath which the remnants of a peat fire still smouldered, and took down an old creased black-and-white photograph. It showed a young eagle on some grass with the croft in the background. The eagle had a broken wing. And the old man said to himself, 'Aye, I knew that was a mistake. I always

knew it wasn't right. But I didn't know how to listen to the
Stones or the wind then. I should have given her time to get
better. She'd have been all right.'

He went to some hooks by the croft door and took down a
heavy, lined anorak which he put on. He put on a pair of
wellingtons and tucked his trousers into them. Then he
stepped out into the night and walked slowly over the
moorland to the Stones of Callanish with all the confidence of
someone who has done it many times before. He had often
felt the power of the Stones before but this night it was
strong, so strong that the cold night and the breeze did not
trouble him.

He stood among the great Stones unafraid, their shadows
friendly, hiding only ancient secrets that would not harm a
man or eagle. He knew the ancient legend and he believed it.
Legends tell many truths.

Then he stared south into the darkness of night, breathed
in the fresh sea air, shivered a little and pushed his gnarled
hands down into the pockets of his anorak, and whispered
into the night, 'I'm going south to London. There's a calling
for me to go down there, but don't ask me why.' And before
he left the sanctuary of the Stones he turned to them as if
they were a person and said with humour and good nature
in his voice, 'It's no good asking *you* why because you'll not
say. You never do!'

                              *

Night and day, night and day, and a growing certainty came
to Minch that her instincts were right and that all would be
well. And strangely, her feeling passed on to the others.

More visitors came to the Zoo than ever they remembered,
staring particularly at Creggan, as if they thought he was
special. Queues of them, most with the black clicking
boxes, all pushing and chattering so the Men had to erect a
special barrier to stop them coming too close.

But Minch did not mind. Creggan had come back and set

in motion a chain of events that would mean these wasted years were nearly over now. They were eagles and would behave like them: proud, fierce, independent and certain.

So they ignored the visitors, staring out over the heads, grooming their wings, eating their food aggressively; eagles to be feared, not eagles to be idly stared at.

*

The Zoo had seen nothing like it for years.

The crowds poured in to see the returned eagle and at the weekend queues formed outside the Zoo, an unheard-of event in November.

But excited as they were, there were some who filed by the Cages who were shocked by the smallness of them, and who were sorry to see that such a proud creature, whose original escape nearly two years before had thrilled the nation, was now in a cage again.

Mr Wolski might have been angry with the visitors who came merely to stare in fascination at a great and healthy eagle caged up once more, indeed he thought he ought to be, but for some unaccountable reason he felt cheerful and in good spirits and bore no one ill-will. So much so that one day soon after the eagle's return, and even though it was raining heavily and even the most enthusiastic member of the public preferred to remain indoors in the lower mammal house and the Aquarium, he decided to sit under an umbrella and eat his sandwiches. It was cold and wet but it didn't matter. He felt like seeing his old friends the eagles and he felt they might like to see him.

So it was there later, when the rain had cleared and only a few drips fell from the upper edge of the Cages, that an old man found him. A healthy old man with a rugged red face and wearing an old anorak and looking half-way to being a tramp.

He came down the path by the other aviaries and over to the Cages. He walked along them one by one, staring up at the eagles until he came to the female golden eagle. He stared up at her a long time, a very long time, and it was then that Mr Wolski noticed him. His wavy white hair contrasted with the black bars of the cages.

The man turned slowly towards the bench where Mr Wolski was sitting and came over and stood right in front of Mr Wolski and looked at him.

'Mr Helmut Wolski?'

Mr Wolski stood up but the man waved a hand and they both sat down.

'I am glad to meet you, Mr Wolski. I read about you in the newspaper. They said at the gate that you might be down here but I think I might have found you here anyway even if they hadn't told me.'

Mr Wolski stared.

'What you said . . .' began the man, looking sadly towards the Cages.

'Ah, yes,' said Mr Wolski, 'imprisonment. I do not like it you know. This . . .' And he waved a hand towards the Cages.

'But you like animals, wild creatures?'

'Yes. Most certainly. I like *them*.'

The stranger looked at Mr Wolski, who found that his eyes were a mysterious sea blue with a hint of that peaceful grey that stirs in the sea after a storm; and Mr Wolski found himself beginning to talk of things he had forgotten and of a life that he had thought was passing him by. He told the stranger of his imprisonment in the last war, of his coming to Britain, and of the long years since, when he had sought a peace he could not find. He told him of his desire to leave the Zoo but of the difficulty of ever finding work at his age . . .

'How old are you?' asked the stranger.

'Fifty-seven,' said Mr Wolski, which was what his natural-ization papers said. It was good enough.

'Fifty-seven!' exclaimed the stranger. 'But that's young and you have been speaking as if you were an old man! Why, I was beginning my life then!'

Mr Wolski sighed and nodded and found himself talking more – of his small cramped lodgings, of the money he had saved and his dream of a house away from London . . .

'Why, look at the time! I really must go now, so late . . .' The old man got up abruptly and reached out his hand, and smiled a smile of warmth and friendship of the kind that Mr Wolski himself might have bestowed upon the few people in the world he called his friends, and said, 'It has been a pleasure, a very great pleasure. I was right to come this long way to talk to you!' Then he was off.

'But who . . .?' But he was gone even before Mr Wolski could ask his name.

Later one of the gatemen was passing Mr Wolski and called out, 'Did he find you?'

'Who?' asked Mr Wolski.

'The old chap with white hair. Told him he'd find you down near the Cages.'

Mr Wolski nodded. 'Who was he?' he asked.

'Why that's Andrew Simms, *Doctor* Simms. Used to work at the Zoo before the war. But retired early as they say and has run an animal sanctuary in Scotland ever since.'

'Where in Scotland?'

'At a place called Callanish.'

17

Over the following days interest in the returned eagle increased even more, and by the weekend the queues of people coming to see him were huge.

But by then criticism was mounting as well, and questions being asked, for although there was no doubt that the way in which the eagles were kept was kind and professional yet many people were distressed to see the cramped conditions of the Cages.

There was an article in one of the biggest Sunday newspapers on conditions in British zoos with grim evidence of mismanagement and cruelty in smaller zoos without the resources and expertise of London Zoo. Pictures of eagles, of distressed monkeys, of bored tigers, coupled with the revelations in one newspaper of a former zoo employee about conditions in one particular country zoo all added to the sense of outrage and concern that the remarkable return of one single bird of prey to the nation's capital had created.

The fact that there was no measurable evidence whatsoever of stress or unhappiness in the eagles in London Zoo itself did not stop many feeling upset by what they saw on their visit.

Staff were asked to work overtime at the weekends to help keep control of the huge crowds, so Mr Wolski was there on Sunday afternoon when a group of militant animal lovers staged a protest outside the Cages themselves, distributing leaflets to the general public.

Mr Wolski did not like it; he might not like the Zoo himself but he knew that treatment was fair and that most of the animals in the Zoo would long ago have died if they had been left to fend for themselves in natural surroundings. But he also felt that five years' freedom might be better than thirty years' imprisonment.

But he was very careful not to talk to anyone about his feelings, least of all newsmen, because he had got into a lot of trouble from the Curator about having his picture taken and published with things he had said.

'I realize that you did not know who it was who was talking to you, Mr Wolski, but there are people in the Zoo who are very upset and angry about it. You have a loyalty to us, you know. If people are going to talk to the press it has to be done officially and through the proper channels . . .'

Upset and angry! That Sunday, Mr Wolski could not but think to himself that having all these people outside the Cages was going to upset the eagles, and not help *them*. So he did his best at least to stay away from the area of the Cages. Even so, with all the hubbub of people and press going on he had the feeling that somehow a crisis was looming, though what its nature was likely to be he did not know.

*

The eagles had watched all these goings on with indifference. They too could sense crisis in the air but so confident and at peace with herself did Minch seem that they believed that whatever change it would bring was not dangerous for them.

Yet as the days had gone by they had begun to lose heart a little, for it is hard to sustain hope that something is going to happen when day after day nothing much does. But for the time being they took their lead from Creggan, who chose to ignore it all.

He stayed at his stance and stared out over the visitors' heads. He fed only occasionally and often backed into his shelter out of sight. He calmly watched the last of the migrant starlings diving and playing at the stump of wood near the front of the cage on which he himself had so often placed his food.

But though he seemed indifferent, he was not. It was still mild for November and the skies above the trees of Three Island Pond were gentle and attractive. Although he had confidence that this imprisonment would not go on for ever yet there were moments when panic overcame him and he wondered how he might escape again.

It was at such moments that he noticed Slorne come near to his side of her cage as if she knew that her presence would comfort him. She was still silent, never having spoken but on that one occasion of his escape, and in a way this helped Creggan because he felt he could talk to her without anyone else having to know.

As evening fell on that long Sunday, and the Men thankfully started to shut down the Zoo for the night, Creggan whispered to her, 'You've felt panic-stricken about how long you've been in the Zoo, haven't you, Slorne? Yet you came to terms with it and learnt to find some comfort here. I wish you would talk to me about it. I wish . . .' but Slorne just put her head on one side and stared gently at him, her sympathetic silence far more comfort than words would have been.

Later that evening Minch spoke to Creggan.

'Do not lose heart, Creggan, for I knew that under the proud indifference you have shown to the visitors today you must feel fear. Have faith as I have had all these years; trust in the powers of that place that sent you back here. Listen for the sound of the sea and the wind and make that sound come true.'

'What do you mean?' asked Creggan. 'You often speak so strangely these days.'

But she was silent, her old wings hunched forward in the gloom, and her aged face staring out through bars she could never escape from. She stared as if she saw something, as if a power would come.

'What is your name and where are you from?'

She whispered the words to him again, as she had often in the past.

'My name is Creggan and I am of Wrath.'

'Of what kind are you?'

'I am a golden eagle.'

'What can you hear?'

Darkness was falling, and winds stirring, moving the old trees above them into stresses and whispers.

'I hear the wind in the trees.'

'Listen, Creggan of Wrath, listen harder.'

Creggan listened and stared forward into the night, and then up above to where the trees branched and bent into the night sky. Wind stirred in them, wind spoke with them, and he could hear something through it, far beyond it . . .

'I hear the sea where it runs on a familiar shore. It runs in the darkness where Faele and my son Creag wait. It runs eternally by night and by day, racing and roaring, whispering over beaches; I hear the wind run over the rough sea and up the lochs to Callanish where the Stones stand.'

'Tell me of our lore, Creggan of Wrath. Tell me of the Stones and what they represent.'

Her voice was the same as it had been when he had first heard it; troubled and in pain. He sensed she was straining to call up a power and that she needed his strength and help. He sensed too something else, something was calling to him, bringing help that in turn would help Minch. So he began to talk of Callanish, and invoke its power.

He spoke of the sacred site before men came when eagles flew over its open space; he spoke of the coming of men; he spoke of the fight between men and eagles and of the making of the Stones. He spoke in the words that Minch had used, and which his beloved Faele had used as well: ' . . . all the men and the eagles had disappeared. In their places were great standing stones . . . pointing for ever to the sky. They formed a great circle around the very centre of the site itself, and long lines across the moor, pointing to the north, south, east and west, that all who saw them would remember that Man and Eagle should be as one . . . as one, as one.'

Though his words were only whispers out into the night, yet they seemed to bring a power about the Cages which many of the eagles there felt and which kept them awake, waiting, waiting . . .

*

Footfalls in the night. A gloved hand on a metal fence. Eyes that look from shadows for danger. Climbing up and over. Trees above, which creak and whisper in the night. The howl of a wolf.

The Cages looming in darkness as a shadow hides in their shadows, and slinks on to a path and by a familiar bench lit only by the night light of a lamp four hundred yards away. The clink of a key. A Man in the shadows.

Minch saw him. Creggan heard him. Slorne, Kraal, Woil . . . they knew he was there. One of the Men, one who hesitated and was afraid, one they knew only slightly. Young, new, eager for action, unwise, as Creggan had once been. As they all once were.

The shift of talons at a stance. Eagle eyes watching in the night.

Key in a cage door lock, a door swings open and stands free. No movement, nothing. Then another. Silence. A third. Doors stand open and the Man moves on. Leaflets flutter to the ground.

Somewhere a lion groans. A shadow crosses the distant light, a watchman coming near. Hands at Creggan's cage door. A key turns, the door swings free. At Minch's; at Kraal's; at each one of their cages in turn.

Footfalls in the night. Danger coming nearer now. The Man slips back into the shadows behind the Cages and over and out into the Park night. No word spoken, no encouragement given. Just some open doors on to a world of sky and wind and the chance for an eagle to decide his own fate at last if he wishes; for that is the true nature of freedom.

*

Creggan was the first. Out into the night and freedom and on to the bench. Waiting. No word, no encouragement. Slorne next, no hesitation before the great sky above. Out to where Creggan had taken stance.

Then Kraal, but with the watchman coming nearer, walking slowly on the path. Moments to go before he saw the open doors.

Others hesitated, none came out. Minch inside and Woil on the brink, afraid to come, afraid. Creggan went to his cage door and whispered: 'You helped give me courage once and now I give it to you. Come, Woil, and join us. Come now. COME!'

The bend of a wing, the thrust from a stance, and Woil was with them, four great birds of prey waiting.

Then Creggan went to old Minch's cage.

She was there staring out through the open door, only feet from freedom.

'Too old, Creggan, too old,' she was saying. 'Can't fly now. Too old to change.'

Creggan saw her fear and understood it well. She who had given so much courage to others and had shown each one of them how to survive this place, might she not feel fear before the open sky?

He went into her cage. He who had never touched her. He went up on to her stance and she was whispering, 'No, fly off now, Creggan, leave me here. I will be slow and make danger for you. Even now . . .' and the Man was coming, only yards from the beginning of the Cages and any moment he would see the darkly opened cage doors.

Creggan went close to old Minch, his young wing to her old and faded one, and he whispered, 'The others know you are of Callanish. They know you are of the greatest of our kind. Lead us now, Minch, and we will follow or I shall stay here with you and be caught again.'

'No no. *You* must go, Creggan, but for me it is too far now . . .' began Minch.

'If you stay, I will stay. I made a vow and broke it once. I will not break it again. You must go before me.'

The sound of the approaching watchman was getting louder. Soon, in seconds only, he must see the open cage doors . . . yet Creggan spoke calmly, softly, for he understood well Minch's fear.

'You have the strength to take the freedom that you have longed for. You gave me the strength to do so. Lead me, Minch, for you are of Callanish, and my kind, and my kin honour you. Faele and Creag, they wait to welcome you. The winds of Callanish wait to put their power again in your great wings.'

'Callanish . . .' whispered old Minch, as if it was a distant unreachable dream . . .

'Come on, Minch!' said Woil urgently from the benches opposite the Cages. 'The Man is nearly here and he will see . . .'

'I will not leave without you,' said Creggan again, in a voice so sure and certain that she knew that it was so.

Then it seemed that the night was filled with the sound of a running tide, of the rustling of duneland marram grass, and of the sound of eternal winds among the dark shapes of ancient Stones as, for the first time in over thirty years, Minch raised her wings at last towards an open sky.

One final time she cast her old eyes over the cage that had been her prison for so long, and she said boldly, 'I told you once of the greatest danger in this place – security, easy food, it robs eagles of their strength. Well, it has not quite robbed me of mine yet. My homesite is Callanish and I think perhaps now the time has come for me to return there! So let us leave!'

With that old Minch pushed herself off her stand and out through the open door of her cage into the night; she held her wings proud and overflew all the others, and with Creggan at her side to guide her, she circled above the Cages and they followed her, a great flight of eagles out into the night sky.

A watchman came to the Cages and saw and heard a rustling of wings disappearing into the night and saw the open doors. He ran desperately forward to find doors opened, eagles gone. But most had stayed, too frightened to fly out into the open air. He closed the doors quietly one by one so as not to frighten out any more of the birds and then ran to raise the alarm.

*

Footfalls in the park. Night. A gloved hand on Park railings. Over, and out.

18

The first Mr Wolski knew something was wrong was the following morning when he was walking up round the edge of the Park to the entrance to the Zoo and he saw two police patrol cars parked outside, and several policemen standing in a solid huddle out of the November rain.

They stopped him at the gate. Him, Mr Wolski, who had worked there for over thirty years.

'Your name?'

He gave it. 'What is wrong?' he asked.

'The escape, sir, the eagles.'

The officer spoke as if he assumed that Mr Wolski knew what he was talking about. Mr Wolski looked blank.

'Eagles, sir. It was on the radio news this morning.'

The officer stared piercingly at Mr Wolski, who had once before, in the war, had police look at him in that way; it was a look that said they didn't believe anything he was about to say.

Mr Wolski said nothing.

Other Zoo staff were being stopped and questioned at the gate and there was an air of suspicion, upset, loss in the air.

The Zoo Curator was there and was talking to officers and looking at Mr Wolski. Mr Wolski decided to get on with his work but another policeman stopped him from going anywhere.

'Do you mind waiting, sir?' They were very polite.

But after a while the Curator came over.

'What is happening, why are they stopping me working?' Mr Wolski asked him. 'What eagles have escaped?'

The Curator looked relieved.

'You don't know about it?'

Mr Wolski shook his head.

'No, Mr Wolski, I don't believe you do. I didn't really think . . .'

'What?' asked Mr Wolski.

The Curator shook his head. Then he said: 'Five eagles have gone, Mr Wolski, including the golden eagle that returned. Apart from him there's the fish eagle, the tawny eagle, the buzzard.'

The Curator paused and gave a slight smile.

'And *your* eagle, Mr Wolski, the female golden eagle.'

The world seemed to stop for Mr Wolski. *She* was gone. She was no longer in that cage. She was . . . free? Or taken by someone who had a grudge against the Zoo?

'We're not certain, Mr Wolski, but we do not think they were taken. There were leaflets of the animal rights group who demonstrated here at the weekend left behind and since they clearly had a key we are sure it was done with help from someone working for the Zoo. That's why the police are here. Fortunately most of the eagles stayed where they were. Someone doing night rounds came just in time to see the five of them fly off. We've got keepers out in the Park but have seen nothing so far . . . and in this weather . . .' The Curator looked out over the Zoo at the grey skies and cold rain that was lashing down. 'It is a terrible, terrible thing. The chances of the birds surviving are very low. It is a terrible thing.'

In the days that followed there were so many more questions, more newspaper stories, more speculation. And though the Curator did not believe Mr Wolski had done it there were those in the Zoo, those who had watched him over the years sitting on his bench at lunchtime opposite the golden eagles and who had read what the newspapers had quoted him as saying about eagles in captivity, who believed that Mr Wolski might well have been involved.

The eagles had completely disappeared. Unlike that first

escape when the male eagle stayed in the Park, this time they had vanished. The fact that the weather turned bitterly cold and the first sleet of winter fell within twenty-four hours of their escape, made it harder to see them.

But two, three, four days passed, and nothing seen. The newspapers called it the 'Great Eagle Mystery' and began to discuss the possibility that the birds had, after all, been stolen rather than released.

For Mr Wolski life became difficult. People at the Zoo increasingly suspected that he had had something to do with it, despite the fact that the Zoo Curator himself vouched for his honesty. He might not like the Cages, said the Curator more than once, but Mr Wolski was a man to tell the truth.

Then, four days after the escape, a reliable sighting was made. It was on the evening television news: two 'huge birds' had been seen in a field on top of the North Downs of Kent. Mr Wolski got down the atlas in which he had marked the previous escape route and found the North Downs. It seemed a long way from Scotland to him. He stared at the atlas and found his eyes wandering up the length of the British Isles, stopping on the low hills of the south-east, rising along the Pennine Way, travelling ever northward to Scotland.

He found Cape Wrath where the male eagle came from. His eye travelled westward over the sea to the Isle of Lewis where the other one originally came from. Only two names were marked on it: a small port called Stornaway and a place called Callanish.

The television news blared on, but Mr Wolski had eyes for nothing but the map of the British Isles. In thirty years he had never really looked at it carefully before. How much land London took up! How far it was to Scotland! How much of this country was there which he did not know; how little had he seen of it in all the years he had been there!

He turned the television off and sat in his tiny room. How small it was, how confined. It was dark outside and the window rattled with the wind. Bitter weather. She was out in it somewhere, free to find her own way now. And he was still here, where he had been for so long, but there was nothing to hold him back now. He had very few friends, and few possessions. It was as if they had all been taken from him a long time ago and he had never quite learned how to find them again.

He went to his bedroom and opened the window on to the wintery night. Cold air blasted in at him but he did not really notice it. He was staring at the glow of the lights of London on the night cloud above. He had made a vow that when she was free he would leave the Zoo and she *was* free now.

Decisions are strange and difficult things. The need for them may be obvious, but making them is hard and may take years of thought and doubt. Yet the moment they are made it all seems so simple and so quick. And the release from the dithering and doubt so great.

So, standing there at that chilly open window, remembering a vow he had made at that same window years before, Mr Wolski finally made his decision to leave the Zoo. Just like that, and whatever the consequences. He had enough money saved to survive for a while; he was only fifty-seven, as that strange old man he met by the Cages had pointed out. No, he did not want ever to work in the Zoo again. Tomorrow he would go and see the Zoo Curator and he would hand in his notice.

Mr Wolski slept that night as deeply as if he had reached the end of a long journey and was safe home at last. His alarm rang and rattled a full minute before it dragged him awake. He got up into a room that was bitterly cold because he had left his window open and there was a November gale blowing, but he felt like a young man again.

He arrived at the Zoo, went to the offices before even putting on his overalls, and asked to see the Curator. He told him of his decision and though the Curator tried to change his mind he soon saw that Mr Wolski had decided.

'It's to do with this escape and all the things being said isn't it, Mr Wolski?'

But Mr Wolski only shook his head.

'It is more than that,' he said. 'So many . . . things . . .' – words failed him, not because he did not have them but because he had no real wish to try to explain – '. . . all these years . . . I have been a prisoner until last night.' The Curator looked blank and concerned, and Mr Wolski finally simply smiled at him and said, 'Now I am free you see. Quite free.'

The Curator stared at him, only half understanding his words. He saw before him a kind, hard-working man who had given his best years to the Zoo and who, unlike some of the younger workers, had never been late, always done his job properly and was kindness itself to those animals he came into contact with.

'Mr Wolski, I will do all I can about arranging for your pension to be paid, though it won't start until you reach the right age, which I'm glad to say is a good way off yet! But have you thought what you are going to do?'

The Curator looked out of the window of his office to the bleak scene of the Zoo, across whose cages and enclosures cold rain swept in grey flurries and huddled figures ran for shelter. It was so dark that in some offices lights had been put on, and in one they included colourful Christmas lights, though the holiday was almost a month away yet. But somehow their gaiety made the Zoo look even more depressing than usual.

'It's not a good time of year to be looking for a job,' added the Curator. 'Christmas . . . high unemployment . . . never a good time.'

Mr Wolski sat silent. Then he said, 'Do you think that eagle thought what she was going to do when the door of her cage was opened and she flew up into the sky? Like her, I will know what to do when I get there.'

The Curator wanted him to work for a full month, but having made his decision Mr Wolski wanted to leave as soon as he could, and since he was paid on a weekly basis they agreed he should leave at the end of the week.

Three days later, a day before he was due to leave, he was called over to the offices and given an envelope by one of the secretaries. It was a letter addressed as follows: 'Mr H. Wolski, c/o London Zoo, Regent's Park, London NW1.' But what interested him more, in fact what made him stop still where he was and simply stare, was the postmark. It read: 'Stornaway, Isle of Lewis.'

*

Creggan crouched in the shelter of rain-lashed trees on the North Downs.

'Well!' he said, as cheerfully as he could, 'we've all survived so far.'

But what a miserable sight they made. Slorne and Kraal were both tired out with hunting, Woil was still out in the storm somewhere, and Minch, whose feathers seemed unable to dry out was getting colder and weaker.

Although it had been Minch who had finally led them out of the Zoo, it was Creggan who led them beyond the Park; and although he had wanted to fly directly north the winds had been against them and they had drifted east to these great lonely chalk hills.

At first Creggan had taken the responsibility of finding food for all of them since they did not know how to hunt for themselves. But Woil had soon got the knack and now the other two were beginning to pick it up.

Woil flew in, wet but triumphant. He held a large rabbit in his talons. Of all of them he seemed most at home here but as he had said more than once, his own kind were spread across the British Isles and had the cunning to survive almost anywhere.

'Trouble with you,' he said, addressing the four eagles together, 'is that you're all too *choosy*. Mountains! Deserts!

Moorlands! Sunshine! What's wrong with a bit of English rain and a few rolling hills?'

Creggan laughed, glad of the return of Woil's positive presence, for he had proved his value every mile of the way.

But really his heart was heavy because he sensed that a turning point had come. He wanted to fly north with Minch while Kraal and Slorne felt an instinctive pull south-east across the Continent to the great blue sea, the sunshine and their homeland.

'We cannot tarry longer here,' said Slorne, who now spoke at last, though only occasionally and then in a whisper.

'No,' said Kraal, 'and what's more, if we're going to survive, we must take route to the south or south-east, towards the sun which will warm our wings and give us strength, and if we split up it will make the survival of some of us more likely. More prey, more space, less chance of being seen by Men.'

Minch nodded. 'This time was bound to come. Although I am weak now and cold I know in my heart that the nearer to my homeland I fly the stronger will I get whatever the weather. Creggan too must fly north.'

They all looked at Woil, who was tearing the prey he had into bits and giving some to each of them.

'Well, I don't know. North, south, east or west, it's all freedom to me. But maybe I should fly with you two if you'll have me,' he said to Kraal and Slorne. 'Maybe you could use my hunting skill for a few days yet. Creggan can look after Minch until she's strong enough to fend for herself. Anyway these golden eagles are an exclusive lot – they don't want to be seen flying north with a grubby old buzzard like me!'

'It would be an honour if you chose to fly with any of us,' said Creggan. 'But though Minch is weak, yet I know that I can protect her and that she will be safe.'

So it was decided, and at dawn the following day the five great birds separated in weather that was still cold and bitter, and getting worse.

'May your journey be safe,' said Minch to the three of them. 'May you protect each other well. And may you reach your homelands with peace and wisdom in your hearts.'

Then Slorne came to Minch and spent time alone with her, talking of memories, and saying farewell. Then to Creggan whose silent comforting friend she had so often been.

'Take care, Slorne,' whispered Creggan, very moved to be saying goodbye to her. 'I will always remember the things you taught me without words.'

She stared at him in the calm and peaceful way she always did: 'Your coming to the Cages was a great blessing and an answer to the powers I myself invoked through all those long years. Your sacred site is Callanish; mine is a different place in the great Atlas Mountains. But really they are as one, and as one I shall always think of us in my heart. Farewell!'

Then Kraal made his farewells, and finally Woil. 'Don't worry, Creggan, I'll see them through to the sunshine they keep dreaming about,' he said cheerfully. 'You just get Minch back to her homesite, that's all I ask.'

Then with a flurry of wings the five great birds circled around each other over the Downs, making flights of farewell such as those grey skies had never seen before, and would never see again. Kraal, Slorne and Woil set off southwards, and Creggan and Minch for the north.

*

Despite the blustery weather Mr Wolski took the letter he had received to the Cages and sat down on the benches to open it. Opposite were the empty cages of the golden eagle and the other birds. There was talk that they would not be occupied again; talk of running the Cages down now and building better ones for those eagles that remained.

But sitting opposite them in the damp air, with his face pink with cold, Mr Wolski wanted to remember those long years he had passed here, and a friend, a golden eagle, who had finally gone free. And a friend he was *glad* to have lost that way. He too was on the point of flying to freedom.

He opened the letter with a curious calmness; silly to read it here outside but somehow, with a postmark like 'Isle of Lewis' that did not matter.

He read it quickly and only bits of it sunk in: '. . . Animal Sanctuary . . . I've run it alone for over thirty years now and am getting old . . . you know about animals . . . Callanish Stones are only a couple of miles off . . . not much to offer in the way of money but there's a warm old crofter's cottage you can have which keeps out the gales . . . there are young people who come to help in the summer months . . . kind people locally. When we met I knew immediately that this was why I had been sent down to London . . . always swore I'd never go back to the place . . . Anyway, come and see and then decide. Tickets for train and ferry enclosed . . . I want to hand over to someone who I can trust . . .'

Mr Wolski stared at the signature. 'Andrew Simms' it read. The handwriting was just a bit shaky.

He remembered the old man to whom he had poured out his heart by these same Cages. He looked at the pink railway ticket marked 'London/Ullapool' and the ferry ticket on to Stornaway.

Mr Wolski nodded to himself, put the letter in his pocket and stood up and took a few steps over to the female golden eagle's cage. He reached out a hand and touched it and he whispered so only the rain could hear, 'So you went ahead of me. Well, now I'm coming too.' Then he turned away knowing that he would never sit on that bench again nor have need to stare into that desolate cage, and he walked more and more quickly, with a growing vigour in his step. He was thinking that there was a lot of life left in the world for a man who has his health and is only fifty-seven, and has discovered at last where true freedom really lies.

19

No power, no force, no purpose could have been more certain than that which drove Creggan's wings forward to the north with old Minch at his side.

He marvelled at the frail strength with which she flew, making the winter winds and bleak horizon seem as nothing before her flight. Yet he knew she needed caring for and watching over, and he was careful to make sure she rested and did not get too cold.

'I never thought . . . that an old eagle . . . like me . . . would manage to get . . . half a mile . . . let alone *this* far!' she said breathlessly when they finally reached the great Pennine chain.

'I'm going to see you get all the way!' exclaimed Creggan. 'You will fly into my home territory with strength and pride and give Faele and my firstborn son Creag a sight they will never forget.'

But the further north they got the tougher it became. The weather was bleak and cold, and somewhere along the Pennines they came to the first snow – a grey frozen ice right over the landscape, rather than the soft fluffy snow Minch was used to in London.

Creggan would only advance when they had fed well and were rested and so their progress became slower. Prey was hard to find and Creggan was taking no chances going into the lower dales as he had before.

But where there is wilderness there is life, and Creggan had trained himself well how to find it. A hare, a fox, a crow, even a raven; he took them with skill. At the same time he began to quarter ground for Minch, driving a rabbit or two towards her that she might learn again the skills of hunting.

He marvelled at her good humour as she overshot a rabbit and nearly hit a wall, the fluffy thing running to cover in the snow.

'Well, I'll learn yet. Can't be fed by another eagle all my life!' said Minch.

At stance in the evenings she would talk to him, telling him of chases she had made when she was young over the Callanish moorland, stories of hunts and close shaves with Men, stories such as all eagles tell on a bitter night to warm the heart and keep their wings from growing cold.

The towns got fewer until at last they were far behind and the great moors of the Grampians rose before them as once they had risen for Creggan on his first flight north.

Then they had been soft with the beginnings of spring, now they were bleak with the starting of winter.

'We are nearing our own kind,' said Creggan with confidence.

But Minch did not speak. She was flying back to her homeland at last and words could not express the joy her wings felt. Creggan fell back and let her go forward alone for a time. She had said she would grow stronger as she went north and he saw now that it was beginning to be so. She flew, as Faele had described, with the grace of an autumn sunset and he knew it was an honour to be her protector.

'Do you want to stop?' called out Creggan, for the gloaming was coming over the moor like an incoming tide. But Minch flew on in silence. Far ahead of her the mountains rose massively up, making the foothills they were flying over seem tiny, and the ragged bunches of sheep and occasional cattle on them smaller still.

They crossed a great swathe of ancient pine forest beyond which the ground was desolate and open, a range of black peat and murky lochans with a stunted birch tree here and there the only form of tree life.

Minch slowed. 'This place, these mountains . . . Creggan, my memories did not prepare me for this. Do you know its name?'

'Rannoch Moor,' said Creggan. 'I came this way before. A vicious place too far from the sea for my taste. Come, let's avoid trouble and make route westwards.'

'Trouble?' said Minch.

They heard the rough call of hooded crows somewhere below; then upon the wind came the haunting flute of curlews and the sudden racing of their wings as they broke off low away from the great black silhouettes of the eagles in the lowering sky.

Creggan sensed danger and flew nearer to Minch, soaring higher with her to give them space. Silhouettes . . . threats . . . they finally came over the moor: two great eagles. They stooped rapidly on Creggan and Minch, ready for a fight.

'Your names?'

'Your destination?'

'Your intent?'

Their voices were bullying and harsh and Creggan had heard them before.

He did not argue or even speak; sometimes it is a waste of time. He simply planed his wings, cut over and round, and swung up aggressively towards the female.

'My name is Creggan,' he said, and gave her a buffet such as once she had given him. 'Of Wrath,' he added, his wings magnificent across the sky.

As she spun round helplessly he turned on the male and thrusting his talons forward and surging in flight towards him caused him to lose his line and cut away below.

'My friend's name is Minch and she is of Callanish.'

The Rannoch eagles swung round warily, flying below Creggan and Minch to indicate that they now meant no harm.

But they followed them as if they could not quite believe what they had heard.

'Tell those whom you meet that an eagle of Callanish is returning to her homesite and that she will take passage across any territory she chooses. She is tired, she has journeyed far for thirty years, and she is to be honoured. Tell them too that there flies with her one of Cape Wrath who is strong and fierce and will have no patience with threat or enmity. Tell them to honour us as we honour all who fly in peace.'

And so it was to be. For as the days passed and they got further on with their journey north they found that along their route golden eagles came to see them, but always in peace. They flew at a respectful distance, some in pairs and some singly; some old and many young. For they had heard that an old eagle full of wisdom, whose flight was like that of eagles of old, was honouring their territories and flying home to Callanish. And they were told that with her they would see a young adult male whose flight was strong and protective, and whose eyes and talons were as true as an eagle's should be.

Until at last Creggan and Minch came to the far north-west coast on a day of clear air and distant views. Where two eagles waited for them watching the southern sky impatiently for what they had dreamed for so long might come true.

Faele waited, with Creag near by. Creag, who had grown away from the homesite but had guarded his father's territory well in the long weeks past. He guarded it still, apprehensive of these 'strangers' who others whispered about before they came. The hooded crow, the curlew, the old raven – they told that special eagles were coming; two great eagles who carried history in their flight.

'Who are they?' asked young Creag, mantling his wings.

'One is an eagle of Callanish whose name is Minch; the other is Creggan, your father, whose trust you have honoured.

When they come from the south we will fly up to welcome
them, for they will have journeyed far.'

So came Creggan and Minch out of the southern sky, their
wings carrying the wisdom of age and the strength and
courage of youth. Across the north-west moorlands and along
the winter coasts until they were within distant sight of
Wrath itself.

Then Faele and Creag rose up to greet them in the
traditional and formal way, asking where they were from and
whither they were bound . . .

To which Creggan said 'Wrath' and Minch said 'Callanish'.

Then they flew great flights of joy to celebrate Creggan's
safe return and the real start of Minch's homecoming.

*

The grey sea swelled and the ferry heaved as the landscape of
Lewis came nearer and nearer. It seemed to Helmut Wolski,
who stood on the wet deck to see all he could, that the great
harbour of Stornaway would swallow them up with its cliffs
to the left hand and rocky inlets to the right, and lights
already blinking on, though it was barely three o'clock.

It had taken him three weeks to pack up his things and
arrange to come. Even though Dr Andrew Simms had only
asked him to 'come and see' yet he knew in his heart that he
would not return to London. So he had packed the few
belongings he had, cleaned out the flat for the new people
coming in, said his farewells to those few people he knew,
and got on a night sleeper to Scotland.

A long journey, but for Mr Wolski it had got more exciting
every minute. The further he put London and the Zoo behind
him the freer he felt, and seeing wild tufted duck sheltering
on the lochs near the railway lines, and watching curlew fly,
he felt as young as he had before . . . before the war. The
ferries were infrequent and dependent on the weather but he
got one and now stood looking at the lights of Stornaway as

he approached over the sea. Houses, friendly lights, and a few people waiting to meet the ferry.

Andrew Simms was there with a welcoming smile, a handshake and an old car to take Mr Wolski over the moor to Callanish.

There was a warm peat fire, and a stew on a much-used stove, and around the walls and on the shelves books, photographs, and binoculars, and maps.

'If you like it,' said the doctor, 'and I've a warm feeling you will, then it'll be yours. I'm too old now and you don't want to share your territory. There's a house waiting for me in Stornaway. Each one of us needs space as eagles do, and the chance to open a window or door on the sky when we want to without worrying if someone else is in the draught.

'But take your time, you've plenty of it. And to help you enjoy it I'm going to give you a glass of whisky. Good stuff on a night like this.'

Mr Wolski stared around him. There were things he would do: a bit of white paint here, a tidy up there; things to repair probably. But he knew it was here that he must be.

'In the morning you'll see Callanish. Walk up and have a look. For now there's things to tell you . . .'

So they began to talk as if they were old friends.

'You're very quiet, Mr Wolski,' the doctor said much later, as they stretched their legs before the warm fire and listened to the wind outside.

'I've come a long way and there are many things for me to think about; many things to forget.'

'Aye,' said the doctor, 'I travelled a long way to get here too and there's not been a day I've regretted it. And if ever there has seemed to be, I go to this window . . .' and here he got up and opened the window that faced out on to darkness but for a few distant lights, 'and I listen to what I can hear . . .'

. . . the roar of the sea and the run of the wind and the

sound of space such as Mr Wolski had forgotten that he had ever known; and to the sound of time that marks itself in centuries and sees the truth of what men do.

'Do you know the legend of Callanish?' asked the doctor. Mr Wolski did, for he had read about it before coming. But there are some stories and legends that are best repeated, since they gain a wisdom and a truth in the retelling.

'It's about eagles and men and how they should learn to live as one . . .' began the doctor, as Mr Wolski settled even more comfortably into his seat and stared into the red flames of the fire.

*

It was a magical December morning, crispy clear with a very slight frost on the moorland and a pale blue sky. The sun was rising softly and the cliffs of Wrath looked down at a flat calm sea, and all was quiet.

Across the western sea was an island shrouded in mist and Minch was looking at it from a stance among the rocks.

'Now I must leave,' she was saying. 'I must return to my home. So many years away, so many memories . . .'

Creggan and Faele looked sadly at her for they did not want her to leave. But they had known these past weeks as she regained her strength and learned to hunt again that this day would come. She had told them so much, and had taken a liking to Creag who thought she was the power of Callanish itself and was in awe of her.

'He is young yet, but will be a fine eagle soon,' she had told them.

They were watching Creag now as he tried to soar on the thin air above them but was finding it hard. 'It's a change to see him flying slow for once,' said Minch. 'Normally he flies a bit too fast for me but now he's learning that there are easier ways of getting there!'

Creag joined them, landing a little way off, for he was shy

of Minch and when she was talking to Creggan and Faele he felt it best not to intrude. But this time he came forward.

'Are you leaving, then?' he asked.

Minch nodded.

Creag stared over the calm sea to the misty island which was Minch's home. He seemed to be struggling to say something.

Eventually he said, 'Do you think you'll be all right?'

'Oh, I think so,' said Minch.

'I mean, don't you think you're a bit, well, sort of . . . old to be going off alone somewhere like Callanish?'

Minch did her best not to laugh.

'Why, do you?'

'Well, I mean . . . I was thinking, you know . . . that maybe, just for a bit, because you might need some help . . . well . . .'

'Yes?' said Minch, her heart full of gentleness for Creggan's son.

'Well, could I come with you?' he asked finally.

'Yes,' said Minch simply. 'I would be honoured if you would. Now that I'm getting so old, and my wings so weak, and I probably can't see as well as I used to . . .' she laughed. 'I was going to ask you to come anyway, Creag. It is time you were leaving your homesite and I wouldn't want you to become a vagrant as your parents once were.'

And Creag could only stare at her in stunned silence, barely daring to breathe, he was so full of joy.

'Take care of him,' said Creggan to Minch later, as they said their farewells.

'Take care of *her* for she carries many things in her wings, a spirit all eagles can learn from,' whispered Faele to Creag as they said goodbye.

'I will,' said Creag, proud to be flying as guardian to a Callanish eagle.

Then they all rose into the air, their wings great across the sky above Cape Wrath and with the winter sun turning their feathers to gold.

Far to the west, across the sea, the sun caught at the mists of Callanish.

'By the time we get there the mists will begin to clear,' Minch told Creag.

'We'll see the Stones then, won't we?' he said.

'Yes,' said Minch. And with that she turned west to cross the straits to the Isle of Lewis and Callanish and away from Creggan and Faele, who watched her flight into the distance with great pride, for their firstborn flew protectively at Minch's side.

And Creggan and Faele watched them far into the distance before turning back to their own territory, to think of winter and plan for the year ahead.

*

Mr Wolski stood alone in thick mist among the Stones of Callanish. They rose as great shadows about him.

It had been decided, though really it had never been in doubt, that he was to stay on and run the animal sanctuary. Andrew Simms would be living in Stornaway now and would be there to advise and help. The croft would be Mr Wolski's to do with as he liked, his own space and territory, and he was already finding that there was no shortage of work, or of help, or of friends. They called him 'Mr Wolski' just as people at the Zoo always had and each day as they saw his patience and skill with animals they respected and liked him more.

Now it was a still winter's day at Callanish, with a mist that would clear as the sun rose. Mr Wolski had walked up to the Stones to be alone with them and think of the eagle that, in a way, had led him here.

As he stood thinking there was the slightest whispering in the grass. A tiny flurry of wind, and then stillness again. Silence, and then another touch of wind and the Stones were whispering. The mist stirred and swirled and filled with the diffused light of sun above it. The Stones seemed alive and he stood quite still as if he was one of them.

A flurry of great wings. A shape in the mist, vast and powerful. On top of one of the Stones . . . he moved towards it but it was gone. The scrape of a talon. He turned and saw the shape again, not quite clearly, and now on a different stone.

The mist was filled with light and shapes that moved as the morning wind strengthened and the mist began to clear.

Then suddenly an eagle, old but strong, was there, and her eyes were staring down at him; and he was staring up at her as he had done so many times for so many long years. But no wire mesh between them now; no bars here.

Nothing but great Stones that told a legend, and a thinning mist that filled with light, and the dark great shape of an eagle's wings as she rose into the sky, and was gone.

Much later Mr Wolski walked slowly away from the Stones. The sun was on them now and the last of the mist was clearing over the moor. He turned and looked back at their dark shapes where they stood forever pointing to the sky. Far beyond them across the distant moor, he saw two eagles soaring freely on the wind, their wings caught sometimes by the shining sun.

The sound of a distant sea was in the air, and the wind whispered of freedom in the grass and heather at his feet.

POSTSCRIPT

The individual(s) responsible for the notorious escape of five birds of prey from London Zoo in November 19–7 was never identified, though an animal rights group claimed responsibility. There were no prosecutions.

Of the five birds that escaped only one, the male golden eagle, was positively traced, its appearance being so well known by then that ornithologists working in north-west Scotland near Cape Wrath were reasonably certain they had located it. It was left alone.

No report of the older female golden eagle was ever received and in view of her age it seemed best to assume that this individual did not survive long in the wild. And surely she would have been unable to reach Scotland.

Nor were the other three ever officially traced. However, a year later, in the autumn of 19–8, a group of German ornithologists conducting a count of the annual migration of raptors across the Straits of Gibraltar from Europe into North Africa for the winter sent the Zoo Curator the following report: 'For several weeks prior to our visit, and before the migration flights began, an African fish eagle (*Haliaeetus vocifer*) was positively identified by local bird-watchers in the area – a fact of which we thought you might like to be informed. The probability seems high, in view of the fact that the normal range of this species is south of the Mediterranean, that this was your specimen.'

But the information that really interested the Curator was a story he heard which put a different, and fuller, meaning to the German report. It came in a personal letter from Captain

E. A. Richards (retd), a British resident at Gibraltar and a
friend of the Curator, and a very experienced birdwatcher.
Writing in answer to a letter from the Curator about the
German report he said: 'This bird (the fish eagle) especially
interested me and I was able to observe it several times before
28 September when we are pretty certain it crossed the
Straits. Twice I saw it in the company of a female tawny eagle
(*Aquila rapax*) and a male buzzard (*Buteo buteo*) feeding
together and warding off others. An unusual sight, I think
you'll agree, and a very interesting one in view of your loss.
A great pity you don't ring your raptors otherwise we might
have been certain. On the afternoon of the 28th I observed
the three soaring together for an hour or more until finally
the two African species separated from the buzzard and
joined the general migration south over the Straits, which by
that date was going strong. The buzzard gyred alone for a
long time after the others left until it finally turned back
inland, when I lost it. I would like to think that all three were
your birds.'

When the Curator read this he hesitated a long time over
whether or not to file an official report on it. He finally did
not do so. Instead, he had his secretary take a copy of the
relevant part of the letter and told her to send it to a Mr
Helmut Wolski who lived in Scotland on the Isle of Lewis, at
a place called Callanish.